KRISTOFF

A BLAIRE'S WORLD TITLE

by

MEASHA STONE
USA Today Bestselling Author

GRAY Publishing
by **Anita Gray**

Note to you from the Publisher

BLAIRE'S WORLD is a spin-off series of 7 Dark Romance titles, written by a collection of USA Today and Amazon Bestselling authors, deriving from Anita Gray's Top 20 Amazon Bestselling, The Dark Romance Series.

You do not need to read The Dark Romance Series in order to follow BLAIRE'S WORLD.

Each story in BLAIRE'S WORLD is a standalone within the series, following the journey of a character from The Dark Romance Series, so expect to see some old faces—and some new ones.

The BLAIRE'S WORLD Series can be read in any order.

Anita Gray has had no creative influence over BLAIRE'S WORLD. The storylines are solely crafted by the authors.

BLAIRE'S WORLD has no affiliation to

BLAIR3 or BL4IRE.

If you would like to discover where BLAIRE'S WORLD derives from, you can do so by visiting www.anitagrayauthor.com or by searching BLAIRE on Amazon.

BLAIRE'S WORLD TITLES
BEAUTY
LUNA & ANDRES
DEMETRIUS
SERAFINA
KRISTOFF
EVELINA
OLIVER

THE DARK ROMANCE SERIES
BLAIRE
BLAI2E
THE DARK ROMANCE SERIES BOX SET

DISCLAIMER
COPYRIGHT 2019 (C)

This novel is a work of fiction by Measha Stone. Any character resemblance to people (fiction and non-fiction), places, incidences, or things is purely coincidental.

All rights reserved.

This story may not be reproduced in any form without the Publisher's consent. Doing so will result in prosecution.

KRISTOFF: BLAIRE'S WORLD

From Blaire

Hey you...reader...yes, I'm talking to **you**. If you don't know what BLAIRE'S WORLD is or who I am, then let me introduce myself. My name is Blaire-Markov. I'm a seasoned hacker and combatant who has been subjected to it all: human trafficking, brutal conditioning, and the most depraved forms of sexual abuse. I've lived, loved and lost, but do you know what? I'm still here.

I'm still fighting.

If you haven't read my story already, then pay attention. Luna and Andres, Oliver, Serafina, Demetrius, Beauty, Kristoff, and Evelina, are all connected to my world. Their lives are dark, their journeys are gut-wrenching, and their stories are only just beginning. Prepare to dive into a sphere of pure, untamed, Dark Romance, and don't expect to walk away unscathed.

Oh, and if once you've finished BLAIRE'S WORLD, you think you can handle me, start with BLAIRE, Part 1 in The Dark Romance Series: Bought. Conditioned. Sold to the enemy—who will change my life forever.

Sincerely, the start of it all, Blaire.

KRISTOFF: BLAIRE'S WORLD

KRISTOFF

KRISTOFF: BLAIRE'S WORLD

1

"Seriously? Ten?" I shake my head but hand over the money for my coffee. It's not like I have a choice in the matter. Without it, I'll fall asleep before I get my shot and seeing as there's not another cafe within walking distance, the barista smiling at me with coffee stained teeth will get his money.

I snag the cup offered and inhale the sweet scent of caffeine. It's probably the cinnamon I'm smelling, but I lie to myself that the caffeine will work better if I can smell it, too.

The sun barely shines through the overcast sky, but it's enough to make me put on my sunglasses. It's going to be a long day, and I need to get my head on straight.

It's taken me three years to get this opportunity, and I can't blow it. Spending most of my savings, I've rented a small apartment above a flower shop and have bided my time.

Andrei Dowidoff's home is nearby, a large estate an hour drive from London. It's a damn fortress, but not without its weaknesses. I just need to find them - and someone willing to talk. Anyone at this point would be helpful. I just need a solid interview, just one.

Officially, Andrei isn't being investigated by any department I'm aware of. He's not the main target, but he's a big player.

"Excuse me." An older man with graying hair and deep creases around his eyes touches my arm as I walk past him. "I'm sorry, my car broke down. Radiator trouble, I think, and my cell isn't working. Do you happen to have one I can borrow to call my son? He'll come get me."

I scan our surroundings. The morning rush around the coffee shop has died down and only a few cars pass us on the street.

"Sure." I pull out my phone from the back pocket of my jeans and hand it over to him, unlocking the screen with a swipe of my finger before he takes it.

KRISTOFF: BLAIRE'S WORLD

He thanks me and starts to punch in a phone number while I sip my coffee. His fingernails attract my attention. Trimmed low and clean. Not a spec of dirt or oil on his fingertips at all.

When I turn my gaze up to his face, I find him grinning at me. He shrugs, but before I can question him, thick fabric is smashed across my mouth and nose. A sweet pungent smell invades my senses as I struggle. Arms wrap around me from behind, and I throw my head back, aiming to hit the bastard's nose. But I miss. My vision blurs. I try to hold my breath while I fight to break free, but it doesn't take any time at all for the chemical to take over.

I drop my overpriced coffee. My muscles weaken, become heavy, and my struggles are too pathetic to do any good. The darkness takes over and wins.

Darkness almost always does.

My eyelids are heavy when I try to blink them open. A dense fog still fills my vision, and there isn't enough light to give me any sense of where I am. An itch on my nose becomes annoying, and I try to lift my hand to rub it away. I can't move my hands; they're bound behind me.

Bound, drugged and alone with no idea of where I am or how I came to be here. I force myself to raise my head and get a good look at the room I'm in. My eyes have adjusted to the darkness enough to realize it's more a cell than a room. The floors, the walls, the ceiling, all concrete. A single bulb hangs over my head, but it's not lit. A thin line of light illuminates along the bottom of the only door in the room. It's probably steel enforced.

Shaking my head, a sad attempt to rid myself of the lingering cloud, I try to focus my thoughts. Testing my feet, I realize my ankles are bound to the chair. My shoulders burn from the bondage. A burn I usually welcome, but this isn't a dungeon. And there isn't a safe-word that will get me out of whatever mess I've put myself in.

I inhale a deep breath, choosing to ignore the rotting stench of the room. I need to clear out as much of the chemical from my body, and cleansing breaths are as good as I can do being tied up.

The door creaks when it's opened followed by a bright white light shining directly into my face. I clench my eyes closed and turn my head, not needing anymore discomfort. Booted footsteps head toward me, two sets.

"Good, you're awake," a deep voice says

with a thick Russian accent. I open my eyes and look sideways up at him. He's older than I would have thought from his voice. Thick dark hair with hints of silver at the roots. His mustache is pure gray, and the deep wrinkles on his brow giveaway that he's past his middle age.

I blink a few times, looking past him. Another man, not as old, stands in the doorway, blocking most of the light and casting himself in a dark shadow. I can't make out his features, but his large, muscular build is easy to see.

"I have to say, Danuta, I am surprised you were so easily taken. You've been a thorn in my side for too long, and so easily you were plucked." His accent makes it hard to understand him through my foggy mind, but I'm pretty sure he called me Danuta.

It's probably the drugs he gave me, but I start giggling.

"You - idiot," I laugh and tug at my binds.

I'm rewarded quickly for the insult with a hard slap across my face. The pain radiates through my jaw and makes golden stars dance before me. Grunting, I shake my head. That didn't help clear up the haze.

"Chertovski suka!" He spits on the ground at my feet. My bare feet. I ignore the fact that he's just called me a fucking bitch and concentrate on my clothing, or lack thereof. I'm naked. Completely exposed.

He has my full attention now.

"I'm not Danuta," I state, working my jaw open and closed. I press my knees together as best I can, given my feet are bound spread apart. "You have the wrong girl."

He gets closer to me, and I can smell the cigar smoke on his clothes. His eyes narrow, and he examines my face, grabbing my chin and turns my head one way then the other.

"More light!" he yells over his shoulder and the bulb over me illuminates. I blink several times, it's too much at first, but slowly I adjust, and I can see him more clearly. A deep scar runs across his chin, down his neck. I've heard about that scar. How he got it. I swallow hard. This isn't a little game for ransom.

Fear floods my stomach, but I manage not to whimper when he increases his hold on me. Showing him my fear, letting him see how scared I really am will only fuel him. Monsters like him feed on it.

"Resemblance is too close." He sneers at me, and I swallow back a smartass retort. My wit isn't going to help me now. Not with Andrei Dowidoff. This man has no sense of humor. At least not the usual kind. His idea of a good time is skinning a man alive to see how long he'll stay conscious.

The stories I've heard are enough to keep my mouth shut.

"I'm not Danuta," I say again.

"I would think a CIA *suka* like you would have better tricks than lying about your name." He lets go of my chin only to pat my cheek. "But we'll see. I can easily give you an injection to make you talk. You'll tell me everything I need to know, and you'll be punished for your lies."

The way he says the word *punished* makes my skin crawl. It's not like when I usually hear the word. There's no excitement, just raw disgust.

"I'm not Danuta. I swear it." I jerk against my binds, but all that happens is I make him laugh. "Check my ID. It's in my pants." I look around the cell. "Where are my pants?"

"We did. All of your clothing and that little bag you had were inspected. You carried no ID." He stands over me now, his hands on his hips.

I had my wallet. Didn't I? I had money to pay for the coffee. Shit. I had grabbed the cash from my pocket. I must have left my wallet in my apartment.

"Even if you had it - IDs can be forged," he says.

He's right of course. How many IDs had

I seen in my sister's briefcase over the years? She's been too many different people for me to remember. I have to convince him I'm not her. That he's got the wrong girl and somehow let me go.

"I'm a journalist," I blurt out. "I'm not Danuta. I'm not working with the CIA. I'm writing a story." On him, but he doesn't need to know that. I didn't come to England looking to do an in-person interview.

"You disappoint me," he says, reaching behind him. Producing a knife, I assume he had strapped to his belt, he holds it up for me to see clearly. The blade is wide and jagged. I have no doubt of the sharpness. Again, I try to jerk free, but nothing happens. The ropes dig into my wrists, but I don't put any more room between us.

Pressing the cold steel blade against my throat, he brings his face closer to mine. "I should slice you, from one ear to the other." His breath is heavy with cigar stench, and spittle lands on my chin when he gives his threat. "Maybe I cut you from chin to cunt, instead." He drags the blade to my chin, nicking me with the tip. I clench my jaw but don't make a sound. Any movement could make the knife cut deeper - and the asshole doesn't need my help in hurting me.

"I'm not the woman you're looking for," I say again, softer, avoiding his eyes out of fear that I'll start whimpering like the pussy he probably thinks I am. I'm not trained for this. I can only go on what I remember my sister telling me of her training, little bits and pieces of things I overheard her talking about with her partner when she thought I wasn't listening.

But she never went over what to do if kidnapped by a high-profile Russian sex trafficker.

He drags the knife over my collarbone to my shoulder. "How is it you look like her then, hmmm?" He doesn't let me answer, just stabs the knife into the fleshy part of my shoulder.

I can't keep quiet now, the pain is blinding and quick. I scream out, a ragged sound. Tears form and fall down my cheeks. He pulls the knife out and presses it to my skin, a new spot, a new threat. Blood dribbles down my arm, droplets hit my thigh.

"I'm not Danuta!" I yell in his face.

He captures my chin with his free hand and turns my head until I can see his knife poised at my shoulder again.

"I swear it. I'm not her," I whisper this time. "Please. I'm not her." I plead in my mind for him to believe me. Because I'm not her.

"Tell me then. Tell me how you have her

eyes, her hair, tell me." I can't see his expression. My eyes are focused on the knife, on the wound he's already created. I can't answer him.

"What do you think, Kristoff? Hmmm? Should we dose her with truth serum? Give her to the men? Maybe a dozen or so cocks shoved in her cunt and ass will help her speak?"

"It's worked before," the man from the doorway speaks. His accent isn't as thick, his voice not as heavy, but just as full of authority. He has a hint of control in his tone, unlike Andrei.

"Answer me, *suka*."

"I'm not her. My name is Magdalena," I try again, sniffling and holding as still as I can manage.

He shakes his head like I've disappointed him again. Slowly, with purpose, he pushes the knife into my shoulder. It's worse this way than the stab. I scream, cry out as more of the blade disappears into my shoulder. I try to move, try to pull away, but all that happens is a larger gash.

"I need more than that," he says, starting to drag the knife toward me. He'll flay my shoulder open if he keeps it up.

"I'm a freelance journalist. I'm writing a story on sex traffickers," I cry out when he twists the knife. "I swear I'm not with the

US government or any government."

"You know Danuta then?" he accuses but doesn't move the knife. So much blood covers my shoulder. My stomach swirls into nausea unlike any I've felt before.

I nod. "Stop. Please," I beg, and hate myself for it at the same time. Danuta wouldn't be so fucking weak. She would already be untied and have his throat between her hands.

"Tell me."

Things won't get better once I do. Things could get a lot worse. But the pain is too much.

"She's my sister!" I say with the last gust of energy I have. "My older sister," I whisper.

Andrei yanks my chin back until I'm looking right into his eyes. He's searching me, to see if I'm lying probably. Like he's a detective now. He has to know I'm telling the truth. Danuta wouldn't have caved so easily.

He jerks the knife from my shoulder and a new burst of pain erupts. I scream, burning my throat from all of the yelling. My head drops forward when he lets go of my chin.

"You are a stupid girl," Andrei says with disgust dripping from the words. It's not the first time I've heard it, but it's the first time I've agreed. Coming to Europe, chasing the story, may be the dumbest thing I've done to date.

"Your men grabbed the wrong girl - but I'm the stupid one?" I laugh between sniffles. I've never handled stress well.

"You want a story about sex trafficking? I will accommodate you."

Pain bursts through my head and the lights go out again.

2

"Fuck," I groan, grabbing my head as I wake for a second time. For a moment, I forget where I am, who I'm with, but it comes back. In a rapid flood of memory and pain, it's all clear again.

My shoulder aches, but the pain is much less. I'm lying on the floor, not tied down to the chair anymore. I touch my shoulder and find it's been bandaged. The blood has been washed away from my arm and the rest of my body where it had dripped while Andrei had his fun.

I push myself to a sitting position, hissing at the burn in my wound and lean back against the wall. I'm not in the same room.

The floor is still concrete, but the walls - they're not walls at all. They're bars.

I'm in a fucking cage.

KRISTOFF: BLAIRE'S WORLD

The chill from the floor seeps into my naked skin, sending shivers through my body. Pulling my knees up to my chest, I wrap my arms around them, hugging myself. I try to ignore the pain in my shoulder and look around. There's another cage a few feet from mine, but it's empty. Bare bulbs hang from the ceiling, one in each of the cages and more outside. The bulb in my cage is lit, and one near the door. Even if I find a way out of my cage, I bet that door is locked.

I push my dark hair from my eyes, tucking it behind my ears and move to my feet. I can't just sit here and wait for my executioner to show.

The other bulbs in the room light up, just before the door opens. A man walks in, over to my cage. He stands with his hands flexed at his sides, his shoulders are broad and he's tall. My head reaches his shoulders.

"Move back," he orders, his Russian accent somewhat watered down. I recognize the voice. He was the second man in the cell with me. What did Andrei call him? "Now." He points a finger at me.

I step back until my heel touches the bars at the back of the cage. Remembering my nudity, I fold my arms over my chest and try to cover my sex with my hand.

He pulls out a key and jiggles it into the lock, opens my cage and steps inside. He pockets the key again, and stands with his arms crossed over his chest, just inside, staring at me.

There are no scars on his face that I can see. Square jaw, dark eyes, everything points in the direction of scary, but I'm only slightly nervous. Unsure of what he's here for, and what he might do to me, I keep my guard up, but I don't sense anger in him. Not like Andrei - that man oozes crazy.

Walking toward me, his focus seems to be on my shoulder. I jerk away when he reaches for the bandages, but he grabs my arm in a vise grip.

"Don't ever pull away when I touch you." His voice is dark, deep and commanding. A tone that would have easily made me eager to follow him if we were back in New York and there were dungeon monitors walking around us. But we aren't in New York, and this man isn't a dominant looking for a fun night.

This man is dangerous.

"Don't touch me," I say and pull away again, but his grip is too hard and all I manage to do is hurt my shoulder more by pulling on it.

He shakes his head. With my arm in his grip, my breasts have been left exposed. A fact he capitalizes on. He pinches my nipple, pulling on it until I step closer to him. The burning pain catches me off guard, and I yelp.

He doesn't release me even when I'm practically on top of him. Instead, he leans down, bringing his lips to my ear. "Every disobedience is punished. Learn this quickly and save yourself a lot of pain."

"W-why am I still here?" I ask, choosing to ignore his turn of phrase. It's like someone has told him all of the right things to say, but he's saying them all in the wrong way. Because he's not giving me options, he's not asking me for obedience. He's demanding it, with the threat of violence if I don't follow along. This is not the stuff little subbies dream of.

"You are here with me to be trained," he says like that explains anything at all. He lets go of my nipple, and I hiss again for the new burn that created. "Now stand still and be quiet while I check your shoulder." He gives me a long stare to be sure I'm going to listen before he starts to peel the bandage back.

I can't stomach to see the wounds on my shoulder. Once I see the black stitches, I turn away. Someone stitched me up. And they must have given me pain medicine because it doesn't hurt like it should.

I close my eyes and turn away again when he starts to probe at the edges of the wound. When I open them, ready to tell him off for making the pain come alive again, I realize he left the door to the cage open when he entered.

He's not holding me at all, just probing the damn wound and setting it on fire again. My heart thunders in my chest; I may not get another chance.

"I wouldn't, but that's just me," he says in a low voice.

I don't care about his warning. I bolt outside the cage and head for the main door to the room. My legs are still heavy from whatever sedative they gave me, but my mind is finally cleared.

"Fuck you." I grab for the door handle and yank. Nothing. I yank again and again. "No! No!" I scream and smack the door. It has to open, I have to get out.

I hear a heavy sigh from behind me. Like a parent who's already told the toddler ten times they can't have the candy in the store.

"Glupaya devchonka," *stupid girl.* His voice carries over to me. He hasn't left the cage.

I yank harder, turning the knob, but still the door won't open. Tears cloud my vision, but I shake them away.

"Let me out!" I demand, turning to face him. "Let me go! Now!" I scream, making my throat burn again.

He doesn't move. The asshole looks fucking amused at my demand.

"Come back here." He crooks a finger at me like I'm some dog going to come when he calls.

"No. Fuck you." I shake my head.

"Magdalena, come here like a good girl, and the punishment will be much less." Silk laces his tone.

"Let me go now, and I won't kill you." My promise is given with a heavier feel to it - even though it's complete bullshit.

His lips curl, slowly at first, then he breaks out into a deep, chest rumbling laugh. "Kill me?" He tsks his tongue, still he hasn't moved toward me.

"Yes. I'll fucking end you," I goad him.

His smile drops a fraction. "Come, Magdalena, it will be so much worse for you if I have to drag you back in here."

My hands flex at my sides. If my heart would stop all the thundering in my chest, maybe I could hear my own thoughts. I'm trapped, and no matter all the threats, I doubt my strongest attack would even tickle the mass of muscle that is standing in the cage.

But to go willingly would be giving up, and I can't do that.

His hands move to his belt and the jangle of metal echoed in the room. He pulls the strap free of his pants in one easy movement.

"Come, Magdalena," he says, crooking that damn finger again. "Take your punishment and learn this lesson."

"No." I shake my head, but my lip is starting to quiver. I have nowhere to go. He's going to win this round.

He sighs again.

"If you don't obey me, Magdalena, my father will see your stubbornness as a reason to feed you to his men." His tone softens, like he's trying to reason with me. "After they've all raped you, tortured you, and hurt you, he'll give you back to me and you'll still get the punishment you've earned. And things will be not so pleasant for you."

I swallow back the little whimper dying to come out. He's telling the truth, I'd heard Andrei already make that threat. And I have no doubt it would be easily done.

His finger is crooked, he's still beckoning me. And like a frightened puppy, I take the first step back into my cage. I need to survive. That thought carries me the rest of the way, back into the cell, back to him.

"Good." Any tenderness that may have been there before falls away. "Stay." And I do. I stand, powerless, watching him leave the cage and go to a cabinet at the far end of the room. I can't see the contents, but when he returns, he's holding a set of black leather cuffs.

He invades my space and holds his belt to my mouth. "Open," he orders. If I keep giving in, he'll keep taking, but if I don't - *I need to survive.*

As soon as my lips part he shoves the worn leather between my teeth. "Hold that." He spins me around until I'm facing the bars and can't see him. My hands are yanked out to my sides. Each wrist is cuffed to a bar. I yank instinctively, but there's no give. Did I really think there'd be any?

I bite down into the belt, holding back my plea. It would fall on deaf ears, I don't doubt.

"Open," he says again, tugging on the belt. My stomach rolls with the anger building inside of me. I want to scream again, but I'm not so stupid to realize that won't get me anything but a sore throat.

I press my forehead against the bar. Readying myself. It's not the first time I've had a belting, but that was drastically different. I had power. I could stop it at a drop of a word. I don't think anything would stop this man.

Light fingertips trail down my back, over my ass. His motions stop and run to the side. He's found my scars.

"You've been caned," he says tracing the thin white scars on my ass. An overzealous

Dom and too much wine. It had been a bad night. I'm lucky I only walked away with a few scars as a reminder.

"Yes." I nod, no sense in lying.

"Why?" His question is full of curiosity - the demand isn't there.

I crane my neck to look behind me at him, but all I can make out is his form. He's too busy examining my body.

When I don't answer him, he digs his nail into my ass. "Magdalena, answer me."

"Fuck," I breathe out when he releases my cheek. How the hell to answer him?

"Why were you caned?"

"It was a game, just some fun," I answer, feeling the heat creep up my neck and over my face.

His hands fall away from me and I hear him shuffling behind me, but I still can't make out what he's doing.

The first fiery strap across my ass lets me know exactly what's happening. The next and the one after that come rapid and low. I cry out and try to twist my torso, but there's no getting away from him. The belt lands again and again, on my thighs, on my ass, across my shoulder blades. He works the belting over my entire backside, careful not to hit the tender spots over my kidneys. He's meticulous and careful.

I promise myself I won't cry. I've taken

serious floggings and beltings before, I can make it through this. But I'm a liar. This is beyond what I've ever experienced - and no end seems to be in sight.

I lose count after twenty lashes, and full sobs break loose. If he took a match to me, my skin would feel less burn. Panic builds in me.

"I'm- Oh! Ow!" I scream, looking up at the ceiling. "Please! Stop!" I wiggle without result.

But he ignores me. Another half dozen lashes cross my ass before he ends the whipping.

I suck in a much-needed breath. Tears cover my cheeks, dripping down to my chest. My nose is running, but I don't care. All I care about is getting air.

His absence is short lived. Pressing his body against my back, he pushes me into the bars. A hand dives into my hair, yanking back my head until it's resting on his shoulder.

He licks my cheek. "Your tears are beautiful, Magdalena," he whispers. "If you had come when I first called you-you would have only been chained to the cell. But every misstep is punished. Remember that." His words are cold, clipped.

I nod, still whimpering like a fool. "Just let me go," I say.

"Never." He seals his promise with a warm kiss to my cheek. "Don't struggle against your binds or you'll tear the stitches in your shoulder. If I have to restitch them, I won't grant you the privilege of being sedated. You'll watch every stitch."

Wait. He sewed up the wound?

"Kristoff." His name hits me, finally, I remember what his father called him. "Please."

His hands are on my ass again, making me hiss at the tenderness. He pulls my ass cheeks apart and shoves two fingers into my sex. I bite back the moan at being filled and try to wiggle away from him. I can't help how my body reacts, but I will not allow him to worm his way into my libido.

"Wet. Koroshaya devushka." *Good girl.* He pulls his fingers out and wipes my own juices across my sore ass.

He doesn't say anything else as he replaces his belt and walks out of the cage. I twist, trying to see him. He can't leave me like this, right? I yank at the cuffs, but the throbbing in my shoulder makes me stop.

The brightness of the room dims as the bulb in my cage is the only one left on, and the thunderous sound of the door being shut echoes again.

He's gone.

My chest heaves and tears I didn't think

could still be inside me flow easily.

3

Andrei sits at the dining table with his fork and knife hovering over the pile of sausage on his plate. He's chewing when he notices me enter the room.

"You saw her?" he asks and stuffs another piece of sausage into his mouth.

I wave away the plate being offered to me and wait until the serving woman has left the room before I speak to my father.

"Yes."

"And?" he pushes.

"And I punished her. She tried to escape." I take several swallows of the beer set at my seat. Tricia, my father's personal servant girl, serves him his dinner most nights. She knows what beer I drink, and always makes sure it's at my seat. And I drink it with much appreciation tonight.

Andrei huffs a laugh. "Stubborn bitch." He shakes his head.

"She's just scared." I defend her and take another long pull of my beer. I feel him scrutinizing me but ignore it. My father has his own ways and I have mine. Mine work - his don't.

"She should be scared," he continues. "We need to find out what she knows, how much of our operation does she know about."

"She's just a journalist, Andrei." I lean back in my chair. I've already had her full history dug into. I don't go into anything without as much knowledge as I can get, and training the American girl is no different.

"What have you learned about her?"

"She works freelance, she didn't lie about that. She's not connected to any newspapers or networks. Mostly she writes fluff shit. Celebrity stuff. But she's been researching trafficking for a while. Her laptop is full of information - nothing specifically tying any individuals to anything." I already had the shitty apartment she was living in cleared out. All her things were brought to me.

"She has nothing?"

"Nothing." I nod in confirmation. At least nothing tangible. She knew where my father's main holdings were. Whatever she really knows is locked up in that pretty head of hers, but I'm keeping that bit of intel to myself for the time being.

Andrei will want her questioned by his men if he finds out what I suspect. And I won't allow that. Not yet.

"Then, we'll move forward with my plan." He goes back to eating, and I wonder briefly if he had anything else to eat besides the fatty sausage on his plate. "I want her ready in one week."

"Of course." I nod. Though, I have my doubts about this woman. She has all the right reactions of a captive. Fear filled her eyes when she saw me enter the holding room. I saw the shiver go through her when I touched her. She knew enough to be scared, but she didn't let the fear overrule her need to get free.

If I hadn't been annoyed by her not coming back into the cage when I called her, I would have been proud of her attempt to flee the room. Stupid attempt as it was, at least she tried. The women who cower so easily before me, they disappoint me - and I know they have a harder time once they are sold.

"Why don't you eat?" he asked, wiping his mouth with his napkin.

"Not hungry." For food anyway. My cock is still rock hard after delivering the punishment to Magdalena. It wasn't her tears, though they were fucking beautiful, or her sobs - more like music to me than cries - but her body's response. How soft she went when I finished belting her. She didn't enjoy her punishment - I made sure of that, but her body still reacted. Her pussy had been hot and wet when I touched her, her nipples had been erect, and when I yanked her back against me, she melted into me. My cock won't ignore true submission.

"What of her sister, Danuta?" I ask, needing a diversion from the thoughts of the red stripes covering Magdalena's ass.

"I have that handled. You get this one under control." He points his knife at me.

"That won't be a problem," I assure him. It's never been an issue before, and it won't now. No matter how beautiful she is - she cemented her fate when she put her focus on the Dowidoff business.

"I have a shipment moving tomorrow, I'm heading to London to oversee it." He turns to the door leading to the kitchen. "Tricia, more beer!" he yells.

Tricia, a short, blond-haired woman - no more than twenty - runs in wearing her usual black corset and lace panties my father forces her to wear when serving meals.

She hands him his beer and bows her head, waiting to be released. He trained Tricia himself, to suit his own needs. I know my father, and the look he gives her tells me he's about to demand a service I don't need to witness.

"I'll see you tomorrow, father." I bid him good night and leave Tricia to lower to her knees and service him while he finishes his dinner.

When I get back to my apartment on the estate, I boot up her computer. Magdalena Nowak won't leave my mind. It's tempting to log into the close circuit video feed in her cage, but I force myself not to. I can't go to her again today. She needs to let her situation sink into her mind, because she's going to have a rough time adjusting if she continues to think she can get out of it.

Instead, I dive back into her files. Checking her browser history doesn't surprise me - not after what I saw in her cage. Kink websites, Tumblr accounts, even a few blog posts she'd written herself regarding submission.

I grab a beer from my kitchen and settle in with her laptop.

"Okay, Magdalena, tell me everything about you."

4

Kristoff had cuffed my hands, so I could sink to the floor and sit in my cage. At first, I was grateful to be able to sit, except my ass hurt too much to have any contact with the cement.

I have no idea what time it is. My body is sore. Every inch. My head from lack of sleep, my ass and back from that belt of his. I finally gave in to my fatigue and moved down to my knees, and then onto my ass. As much as it hurt, I couldn't hold myself awake any longer.

When I woke up, I half expected to be unbound. My stomach growls, reminding me I hadn't eaten. Scrambling back to my feet, I relieve the pressure on my sore ass. Surely, there are welts and bruises. The skin feels so tight, I'm afraid it will split if I bend over too far.

I've tried to search the room, but he bound me to face the wall behind my cage. I can't see anything other than cement blocks. And craning my neck doesn't help.

The door opens behind me. Boots move along the concrete flooring, but no lights flicker to life. I look over my shoulder but only see a glimpse of a black shirt as Kristoff opens the door to the cage. Stupid that he locked the cage after binding me to it, but I'm not going to remark on it. I'm going to try something new.

"Tak chto on izbil tebya." *So, he did beat you?* a new voice says. I turn the other way, trying to see this new man, but he stands out of my line of sight. They don't know I can understand them, and I'm not giving them that power yet, so I don't answer him.

A tray drops at my feet. Scrambled eggs bounce, some spills onto the floor beside the tray. An apple rolls to the edge of the tray and off.

"Breakfast," he sneers in his thick accent. "Your ass is redder than the apple." He laughs, stepping closer. His hands on me, I clench my ass and try to twist away, but he's gripping me hard and I can't get free.

"Stop," I demand, but he only laughs.

"Did Kristoff fuck this ass last night?" He pries my cheeks apart and I arch my back, trying to press my pelvis into the bars, away from him.

"Let me go, you asshole." I grind my teeth together. So much for my new plan of playing nice.

His laugh sounds dirty. I cringe when he moves closer to me, his hands moving up my back and around to my front. I kick out at him, but he's already grabbed my breasts.

"These tits." He groans and pinches my nipples.

I throw my hips back at him, trying to knock him away, but he only grabs my nipples harder.

"Fucking bitch," he says in English - probably because he wants me to understand him. "Try that again and I won't even spit on my cock before I shove it in your ass."

I freeze. His right hand has left my breast and his zipper is worked down. His dick presses against my ass and he needs both hands to pull my cheeks apart.

Fuck. No.

I fight back, wiggling and kicking back and throwing my head back trying to hit him or get away. Anything to keep that prick of his from touching me.

"Chto za chert!" Kristoff barks. I don't stop fighting my attacker, because I have no idea if Kristoff is here to help me or him.

"Get away from her!" he yells, and the

man is thrown off me. My foot slips in the splattered eggs and I hit my chin on the bar but recover in time to see Kristoff throw the man to the ground and press his boot to the naked cock lying limply against the man's thigh. "Ty ne trogavesh' menya." *You don't touch what's mine* Kristoff says in a voice so low, so dangerous even I freeze at the sound.

The man glares up at Kristoff but doesn't try to move. He fires off a protest in Russian, too fast for me to catch every word, but I understand enough to know he's insulting me and members of my patronage. Kristoff doesn't defend my honor, simply restates that I'm not to be touched. Because I belong to him.

"She's mine," Kristoff spits, sounding angry. He shoves his boot into my attacker's midsection before stepping away. "Get out."

I turn away, not wanting to see the fury in Kristoff's eyes when he faces me.

He kicks the tray away and uncuffs my hands. My shoulder muscles burn when I drop my hands to my sides. They weren't stretched too far out, but enough that the muscles have tightened overnight. The cuffs aren't removed from my wrists, just from the bars.

"Put your hands behind you," he orders, shifting my position.

"My shoulder hurts." I roll my arm,

trying to work out the tension. Any help I thought he might give is just a dream. He pulls my hands behind me and clicks the cuffs together.

"And whose fault is that?" he growls.

"Well, I didn't stab myself," I retort, instantly regretting the comment as he grabs my ass cheek.

"If you try to run, or escape me while I transport you, the little belting you had last night will seem like a vacation."

I nod, positive he means what he says, and not wanting any part of what he gave the night before.

"Walk." He turns me to face the open door and pushes me with a single finger in the middle of my back. I'm so easily controlled now.

"Where are you taking me?" I ask once I'm outside the room and in a dimly lit hallway. The air is stale, musty.

Kristoff doesn't answer me, just keeps needling my back with his finger. I walk faster, trying to get away from the annoying sensation, but he only quickens his step along with me.

The doors along the hallway are all closed. No windows on any of them. I try to listen for sounds. Are there other women being held captive down here? Is this where they keep the girls before they sell them?

KRISTOFF: BLAIRE'S WORLD

"Shit." I stop walking and shake my right foot. I must have stepped on a rock. Kristoff grabs my arm to keep me steady. Did he think I'd run off, naked and bound? I'm not as dumb as he and everyone else thinks.

"Let me see," he orders, snapping his fingers and pointing at my foot.

"Why?"

He sighs, heavy like he's had enough of me already. He points again.

Bending my knee, I show him the underside of my foot. There's a cut, blood is already trickling down my heel.

Brushing away the dirt as best he can with his fingers, he bends lower to see better. If I was more trained, better skilled, I could use his positioning against him and try to get away.

He pulls the skin of my heel and I see the wound open up and more blood rises to the surface. I hiss and try to pull away.

Keeping his grip on my arm to keep me steady he bends down to the ground and picks up what looks like a shard of glass. It's long and jagged. He pockets it and in a swift movement, he lifts me from the ground and deposits me over his shoulder.

I grunt, as much about his shoulder digging into my stomach as the indecency of the position he's put me in. My hair falls around my face, shielding me from sight.

How can I map out the place if I can't even see it?

"I can walk," I say, trying to buck up and back over his shoulder.

He smacks my ass. Hard. Not a little pat to remind me he's in charge, but a sharp stinging smack that reminds me of how much harder he can go with me.

With my hands bound behind me, it's hard to do anything other than lay like a limp bag of potatoes. Annoying and uncomfortable, but still the bigger problem, the more concerning issue is I can't see where he's taking me. And I have no idea why.

The cement flooring turns to wood stairs then to carpeting. He's taking me through a building. A house maybe?

Men are talking somewhere off in the distance, but no one interrupts our movements. I splay my hands across my bare ass as best I can just in case. Kristoff's chuckle tells me he finds the action pathetic.

Well, fuck him.

I make sure my legs stay clamped closed as he takes me up another flight of stairs. And another.

Where the hell is he putting me? Is he moving me from a dungeon to a tower?

"I don't want anyone inside; do you understand me? I am not to be interrupted for any reason," Kristoff says in Russian.

"Of course," a deep voice responds. I try to look up again and growl, frustrated I can't see anything and have no control over my own damn movements.

A door opens, and we enter a room, an apartment? We could be entering the third ring of hell for all I know. Considering the treatment I've received so far, the idea isn't too far away from reality.

Kristoff flips lights on as he walks farther into a room. We pass a couch. The rug changes from blue to gray. Another door opens. And another.

I'm dumped on to the middle of a bed, and immediately I scramble to my knees, shaking my head to get the hair out of my eyes. It's not long, only shoulder length and thin, so it's not usually a problem. But hanging upside down makes it more so.

"Stay." He points a finger at me then walks back to the door, slamming it shut and bolting it. Who would he need to keep out of the room?

Shuffling on my knees, I move as far away on the bed as I can get from him without falling to the floor. My chest aches from my heart beating too damn fast, and I can't seem to get enough air. I'm locked in a room with the massive man who already has shown me nothing but pain.

He barely glances my way as he moves around the room, opening drawers and digging through them. He slams the last one shut and curses under his breath.

"Don't move from that spot." He jerks his finger at me, like it's my fault he can't find whatever the hell he's looking for. I give him a nod since he seems to require acknowledgment before he gets moving again, and he unbolts the door.

While he's gone, I sweep my gaze around the room. It's just a bedroom. A fucking huge, luxurious bedroom, but just a room. No torture devices, no weapons hanging from the walls. If I'm not mistaken, there's even a walkout patio through the French doors. He took me up two flights of stairs, but were we underground for the first set? How far up are we really?

As I'm trying to figure out how high up of a jump I can survive, the door opens again and he's back.

He ignores me and walks past the dresser through another door that I assume is a bathroom when water starts running. Then a shower turns on. He's taking a damn shower? Now?

I move from my knees to a sitting position in the bed, wincing at the tenderness still covering my entire backside. Even the plushness of the bedding isn't enough to make me comfortable.

I'm just starting to ease off the bed when the bathroom door pulls open again and he calls me.

"What?" I ask, not having heard the last of what he said.

"Come here," he says and crooks that fucking finger of his again. I'm going to break that finger.

"Why?" I tense, knowing if I piss him off, he'll hurt me again, and I don't want to be hurt. But I don't really want to walk into a room that for all I know has been prepped to drown me.

He squares off with me, his dark eyes focused on mine, his jaw clenched. "When I call you, you come. You don't ask questions. You do what you're told." He crooks his finger again. "Here." And points to a spot on the carpet just in front of him.

I roll my eyes. Yeah, I'm not playing this game. Not with him.

"Magdalena, I saw the bruises on your ass and your thighs. They will hurt much more today if I have to take my belt to you again. And I won't go easy on you just because of some bruises - it will be worse because you've earned a second punishment in such a short time."

The way he talks reminds me of a Dom I used to play with back in New York. He was a stickler for obedience. It was fucking hot, I won't lie. But this is different. This isn't just being a good girl to get the orgasm at the end of the night. This is survival.

And I'd prefer to survive.

I slip off the bed and walk across the softest carpeting I've ever felt and stop just short of where he pointed. Some habits are hard to kill, even with his stern glare fixed on me.

"Don't think to win. You'll never win." A clear warning to not push him. "Now, get to your knees."

There isn't a part of my body that isn't aching and moving down to my knees still bound isn't going to be easy - or graceful. The air swirls thick between us, his irritation becoming palpable.

With a heavy sigh, I sink down to my knees. Flicking my head to the side, I throw my hair out of my face so I can look up at him. His jeans are tight around his thighs, and his black t-shirt is snug around his chest. The man is more muscle than flesh.

"I'm going to uncuff you for a shower. Everything you need is already in there. Don't do anything stupid and when you come out, we'll talk."

"I had to get on my knees for you to tell me that?" I can't seem to stop myself.

"You had to get on your knees,

Magdalena, because that's where slaves belong." He says it so gruffly, it's almost hard to understand with his accent, but my body reacts to it easily enough. It comprehends him.

"I'm no one's slave." I thrust my chin up.

He responds with a slow, easy grin. And for a moment, he almost looks pleased. "We'll see about that." He pats my cheek. "Shower."

I'm hauled up to my feet and spun around. The man handles me like I'm a damn rag doll and not a woman. After my cuffs are removed, I rub my wrists. They hadn't been too tight, but it's nice to have my body back under my control again.

He steps to the side and gestures for the shower. It's a walk-in with a glass door that's steamed up. With a quick glance back at him, I open the door and step inside.

The warm water runs over my body, soothing some of the ache from my muscles. I'm deeply aware of the monster lurking on the other side of the door, but I push him from my mind as best I can. This may be the best feeling I have all day and I'm going to enjoy it.

Remembering the breathing techniques I was taught, I take deep steady breaths and let the warm water run over my head. Water runs down my face, over my shoulders. I wonder briefly about the stitches, but shove that thought away and concentrate on my breathing.

No matter what happens next, I will survive. I will find a way out of this fucking stronghold and get free.

"Time's up." A hard knock on the door ruins what tranquility I was able to find.

I quickly wash and turn the water off.

The door opens and he's there again, hovering with a towel. I try to take it from him, but he shakes his head.

"No, I'll dry you." He looks down at the bath mat where I assume he wants me to stand. Fine, if he wants to dry me - go ahead. I have more important things to worry about. Like what he is going to do to me in the bedroom.

The plush towel runs over my body and he makes quick work of the task, only slowing down his movements when he's drying my breasts. When he reaches my sex, he squats down before me.

"Open your legs," he commands.

"I'm fine there," I say, but he slaps my thigh hard. "Fuck. Fine." I move my right leg out and stand with my feet shoulder length apart.

The towel runs up my inner thighs to my sex. I think back to the last time I shaved, not that I should care, but find myself relieved to remember I had taken care of it just the other day.

"You're wet," he accuses with some levity in his tone.

"Yeah. That's what happens when you take a shower." I remark with more snark than I intend. My nerves are running wild and controlling my tongue is becoming harder and harder to do. And it's not helping that my body keeps reacting to him. My pussy is wet; I can feel it and it's not the water from the shower.

"Hmm." He doesn't reprimand me for my remark.

The towel falls to the floor, and he holds my hips. I try to pull back, but he's too strong and his mouth is on me next. His tongue swipes through my folds and swirls around my clit.

I fight back the moan and try to step away from him, but he's just too damn determined. Suckling my clit into his mouth, I let the moan escape. It's been too long since I've been touched like this - have I ever been touched like this?

His tongue is as stern as the rest of him, and he continues to lick and suck my sex until I'm a heaving statue. I want to grip his hair, drag him up and down my pussy, but I manage to control myself enough not to.

"You will come for me," he says and

thrusts two fingers into my passage.

"No." I shake my head, but arch toward him wanting more than just his fingers.

"Yes, you will. And only when I give permission. Come hard for me, right here." He fucks me with his fingers, curling them slightly and hitting the exact right spot. I should pull away now that he's only got one hand on me, but instead, my body leans into him.

He's biting me, sucking, licking, fucking, all the right movements, all the right sensations.

"Come," he orders in that stern tone of his. The one that should send fear through me, but not in this instant. Not when he moans and flicks his tongue over my clit faster and faster while his fingers are pumping in and out of me.

I can't. I can't come just because he said or because he's touching me. I need to get away.

"Come, Magdalena, be a good girl for me."

Oh fuck.

"Your pussy is so tight, so good, now be good too, come for me," he says, and the tip of his tongue touches my clit spiraling me out of control. The waves ripple through my body, from my head to my clit and back. Screams fill the bathroom. Mine. My screams. My hands grab for the wall behind me to keep from falling over.

He doesn't stop, he keeps fingering me until the very last pulse falls away and then he places a soft kiss to my clit and sits back. My chest heaves and I suck in air as I watch him lick his fingers clean of my juices.

I caved.

I lost.

Just like he said I would.

"That's a good slave," he says with a cocky grin and stands up. I think of a retort but find myself swooped up in his arms and carried back into the bedroom.

I'm tired, sore, and hazy from the mind-blowing orgasm he gave me.

After I'm dumped back on the bed, he stands over me with his arms crossed over his chest.

"Now. You'll answer my questions. First - how did you learn Russian?" he asks me and then I realize my mistake.

He's been speaking to me in Russian since he put his tongue on my clit.

5

She's cute. Realization hits her features and she blanches. She thought I hadn't noticed her reactions when she wasn't supposed to be understanding. She'd learn.

Finding that fucking asshole getting ready to rape her had set my nerves on fire. No one but me will touch her. No one.

I could sit and evaluate why I feel so protective over her, but I won't. It would only end badly - for us both. No matter what I feel, she's to be trained and sold. End of story.

"Answer me," I bark at her when she remains quiet. Her mind is reeling, looking for a plausible lie. But I've already figured out one thing about my Magdalena - she's no good at lying.

"I took it in high school," she blurts out

and I laugh.

"You took Russian in high school? In America?"

"College?" She tries again, but her voice is weak.

I take a deep breath. "Your sister, did she teach you?"

"Danuta? No. She—" She looks away from me, like it's embarrassing to speak. "She never taught me."

"You taught yourself then," I say, keeping my voice hard. I have my suspicions, but I'm not giving them away yet. If I'm right, she has no idea.

"Yes." She nods and pulls her knees up to her chest, covering her naked body from me. I sense it's not her body she's trying to hide though, and the part of her she's wanting to shield won't be kept from me.

"Why?" I ask, not really needing to know. None of this is important, and it's distracting me from getting to her training, but I want to know.

"Why did you bring me up here?" she asks her own question.

I tilt my head, examining her features. "I could use the truth serum on you. It would be easier to get my answers." I won't, but she doesn't know that. The serum would make her mind clogged and she'd be useless to me physically for a day. I only have a week to get her ready; which makes every moment count.

Her eyes widen, and for a split second, I see the fear lingering there. Just a brief moment before she covers it up with annoyance. She's tired of threats and being bossed around. Which I find more amusing than maybe I should. After browsing her computer, I know it's what she loves deep down. But she's not in control here, she can't just mutter a word and end all of this. Here, her submission isn't her choice.

"My sister learned Russian for work, so I taught myself." She shrugs like her confession has no meaning, but I know better. I've met her sister. I know what the bitch is like. I've seen warmer temperatures in Siberia.

"How many years older is she than you?" I ask, knowing it can't be many, they look too similar. Although, not so close that my father should have mistaken one for the other. But he's getting old, and it's been many years since he had a run in with Danuta.

"Seven." She rests her forehead on her knees. A rumble from her stomach reminds me she didn't have breakfast. That motherfucker comes back to my mind and I can't wait to put my fist through his face later for his insolence.

"You know what she does?" I ask, though prying into the connection between her and her sister won't achieve my task.

"She—" Magdalena sighs. "She's going to find me. She's going to come here and find me and kill all of you." I hear the desire in her words, she wants them to be true, desperately.

I don't laugh. There's nothing funny about what's going to happen to her once I'm done with her. Letting her have hope would be cruel.

"No. Magdalena, she's not. She's never going to find you. Once I have you properly trained, my father will sell you to the highest bidder. If you obey, if you learn, you'll be lucky and a man who enjoys obedience will buy you. But if you resist, if you don't present well, a man who enjoys punishing girls like you will buy you." I step closer to the bed. "And you don't want that."

Tears build in her eyes, shimmering on her lids before they fall silently down her cheeks. The flush from her orgasm has faded.

"I have a meeting. Rest in here, don't fuck around and I won't bind you, but if you try to escape or hurt anyone that enters this room, you'll be bound and chained." I wipe my hand across my mouth, the taste of her still lingers on my tongue.

Giving her the orgasm hadn't been my original plan, but it seems to have done the trick. She's more pliable, more thoughtful.

"I'll have Tricia bring up a tray of food for you. She won't hurt you, but if you do anything that suggests disobedience, she will tell me." It's true, she will, if I ask her. Even after all the years under my father's control, Tricia will still try to protect those she thinks are innocent. But she's been conditioned never to directly lie. If asked, she will tell the truth.

"I'm not hungry," Magdalena says from the bed, her face is buried in her lap again. Her dark hair shrouds her features. She's going to have a rough afternoon, but it can't be helped.

"Don't be stupid. I can hear your stomach growling from here, and food will keep your strength up. You'll need it." I head to the door and unbolt it.

"I won't eat it," she mumbles.

"If you don't eat, I'll force it down. You won't win these little tugs of wars, Magdalena. I will make you even if I have to sit on you and shove the food down your throat with my fingers, you will eat." Potential buyers will want her healthy - not a bag of bones, I tell myself.

I take her silence as agreement and leave her alone in the room, locking the door from the outside. No one can go in or out without my key.

Once I get Tricia working on more food for our newest captive, I search out the bad guy. It's time we have a talk about touching other people's things.

6

It's evening before I hear the lock on the door turn again. Earlier, a young woman, Tricia, brought me a tray of food. Fresh fruit, toast, an omelet, and coffee. I tried to speak to her, to get some information, maybe help, but she only shook her head and kept her lips sealed.

I scramble from the bed and brace myself. If it's not her, it could either be Kristoff or one of his men. I won't be caught off guard a second time.

Kristoff steps inside and stops short when he sees me, fists up, legs spread, ready to battle. He rolls his eyes and shakes his head. Obviously, I'm not as intimidating as I feel.

"You're dressed. Why?" he asks while bolting the door.

I drop my hands to my sides and stand

upright, tugging on the t-shirt I wear. His pants were all too big on me. So is the dark blue t-shirt, but at least it covers me.

"I was cold," I lie. I could have just snuggled up under the covers. The linens looked so soft, so comfortable, I was afraid I would fall asleep too deeply to hear if the deadbolt turned again.

"Lie again, and I'll hang a weight from your tongue." His words are chilled.

"I wanted to get dressed," I say and hug myself around the middle.

"And you think your wants are meaningful here?"

I wish I could see past the darkness in his stare. He can't be so black and white, either angry or pleased. There has to be a middle ground there somewhere.

"I think you left me in a room full of clothes, and I had none. So, I fixed the problem." I manage to keep most of the sarcasm out of my tone.

"You weren't told to get dressed. You only do what you are told to do, and don't do what you are told not to. This is the first rule you will learn." He pockets the key and leans his hip against the door. "Remove the shirt."

"I won't be trained like some fucking animal. I will not let you sell me." I say the words, feel the heat in them as they leave my tongue, but my insides aren't so confident. There's no one here to stop them, to help me.

He doesn't bother to respond. He walks to me and rips the shirt neckline hem down the middle. In one quick motion, he spins me around and yanks the shirt down my arms, the fabric burning my skin as it's pulled free.

"You don't *let* anything around here. Here, you do as your told. I'm getting really tired of telling you that. You need to accept your place, accept what's happening or it's going to be so much worse for you." He grips my hair, yanking my head back and bringing his face close to mine. "Don't make this worse on yourself."

His words remind me of a parent pleading with their child to just behave, because they don't want to punish them. But that can't be true for Kristoff, this is what he does. His whole life is making women do things they don't want to do and punishing them when they don't.

"Fuck. You," I say through clenched teeth. I think being left alone for too long has given me a new bravado. I want out, and I'm not going to be a pussy about it. I will not let this man scare me, I won't let him train me and sell me like I'm nothing. Because I am something.

"You haven't earned a fucking yet." His lips curl slowly like he's found a new way to piss me off.

Gathering as much saliva as I can, I spit it in his face. It lands across his eyes and nose, dripping down his cheek. I gasp at the sight, knowing it was too far, too much. He'll have to retaliate.

With his free hand, he wipes my spit from his face and smears it across my chest. Struggling only hurts me, his grip too tight at my scalp, but at least I try. I have to escape. I can't give in.

"Fine. You want a fucking." He drags me to the bed and shoves me down over the side. His hand smashes my face into the mattress; his knee jams between my thighs, wedging them apart.

"No!" I can't get a good enough grip on the bed or gather enough strength to push him off me. Like a wild animal, I shove and kick and fight him. This isn't going to happen. I won't let it.

"You wanted this. Remember that. You asked me for it." His tongue runs along the shell of my ear, his words penetrating deeply. He's too big, I can't move him. Doesn't stop me from squirming though.

His hand runs along my sex, running around my clit. The stimulation is there, but my mind rejects it. "No!" I scream again and increase my struggles.

"Spit for me again, Magdalena. You did so good the first time." His angry growl penetrates me. His hand appears before me, his palm waiting for me to spit in it. "This is the only lubricant you're getting so make it good." He shoves my head again as if to remind me of his strength. I can barely breathe with him crushing me like his.

"Please. No." I suck in a breath when he lets up the pressure on my back, but it's short-lived. "Don't."

"Spit or suffer more. Your choice." He nudges my chin with the edge of his hand.

Thoughts spin through my mind. If I spit, I'm condoning this, I'm giving him permission. If I don't, I'm going to make it harder, he'll hurt me. This is what the lesson is all about, right? Giving into it, and accepting my fate?

He growls, "Upryamaya devushka," *stubborn girl.* He shoves me again and forces his hand into my mouth. Fingers encroach too far back, and I gag. Pushing his hand away doesn't work, he's not going to give up until he's ready.

His hand disappears, and his buckle is undone, his zipper rips down and he's muttering to himself behind me. I can't understand him, he's talking too low, too fast.

KRISTOFF: BLAIRE'S WORLD

"Kristoff, no!" I push up again, but he just smashes me back down. If I struggle more, he'll rip my hair out. Switching gears, I rear my ass back at him, then start to kick my legs out.

But he doesn't care. Compared to him, I'm a rag doll.

The tip of his cock penetrates me, and I scream. A long, throat splitting scream as he slowly slips into my body. Too big, I'm too small. I scramble again on the bed, needing to get away, to get him out of me.

He tightens his hold on my hair and has my hip in his other hand, his nails digging into my ass.

"Stop!" I scream, but he retracts only enough to push back in again. The pain blinds me, and I cry out more. Swinging my hands behind me, I only make contact briefly with his arm, or was it his chest. I can't see, and I can only focus on the burn of his cock stretching me from within.

"No!" I yell again.

He's not saying anything. He's not even responding to my struggles. His cock continues to thrust into me over and over again and I cry. Tears pour down my cheeks, soaking the bed beneath me.

"Get off me!" I burst into a new battle cry and flail beneath him, but my strength is getting less as he continues to pump himself into me. If I was facing him, I could claw at his face, but he's behind me. Fucking me like a dog, my face pushed down and my ass high up for him.

"Fuck." I hear him, and he releases my hair to hold my hips with both hands.

Bucking up, I try to get away, but he shoves a finger, maybe it's his thumb, into my ass and I scream again. My throat is on fire, but I keep screaming for him to stop. He's turned a deaf ear to me.

"Keep fighting me, and this will be the hole I fuck next." He wiggles his finger inside my asshole. It's not very deep, just barely penetrating me, but it's enough to send a new tremor of fear through me.

"Stop. Please," I beg, but it's too late. He's already fucking me. He's already inside and taking what he thinks is his.

He's grunting with each thrust. My hips are going to bruise from the force that he's holding me. Pushing up doesn't work anymore, my arms are jellified.

My screams fade to sobs, and I'm left crying into the mattress having lost all that bravado I had when I spit in his face. Only moments ago, but it feels so far away.

The fight hasn't left me, not even with the looming threat of his finger. I can't just let this happen. There's more to me than this.

I kick my legs back and try to throw my weight to the left. A sad attempt to throw him off me, and it fails miserably.

"Damn you," he says softly. He pulls my ass cheeks apart, wide, so wide it feels like my skin will tear. "Stubborn, so fucking stubborn." His words are accusing. Like what he's doing is my fault. Like I brought this on myself.

Maybe I can get to his face if I turn my torso again. But my thought of attack is frozen in my mind when his cock pulls out of my cunt and rips past my anal ring.

He's in my ass.

Shock takes over first, then the burn, the pain.

I scream, louder than before. All sense of fight recedes as my mind can only concentrate on the blinding pain in my ass. He's not gentle. Not relenting. He's a man on a mission. To make me submit to his punishment.

Another thrust, more pain-sharp, unyielding, and he stills. My hands fist the bedding beneath me as he releases his cum into me, filling me. A new pain spreads through me, filling my chest. Rage. Pure raw rage, tampered with the idea that he's still on top of me.

Insults, rants, threats all burn my tongue wanting to escape and fling at him, but I hold back. I bury my face into the covers, humiliated, worn out, used - fucked.

He slips out of me, stands up and rezips his jeans. "Get up." He smacks my ass. "Stand up now," he orders in that steel voice of his.

I want to tell him to fuck off again, but I think I've learned his punishment. He'll just make me. He'll always make me.

My feet find the floor and I manage to push myself to stand on shaky legs. I can't see him well with my hair mangled in front of my face, but that's fine. Looking at him will make me vomit.

"You will remain naked at all times." He pushes my hair away from my face with a gentleness he did not afford me only moments before. "Do you understand me?"

I nod.

"Words, Magdalena. Always words," he corrects me, but the steel has softened.

"Yes."

"Yes, what?" he asks, and I chance to look up at him. Tears still linger on my lids, making his features blurry but I can see the wrinkled brow, the tense lips. He's still teaching me.

"Yes, sir," I whisper, not getting one ounce the satisfaction I've gotten in the past at using the phrase.

"Clean yourself up. I'll have dinner sent

up for you." He looks me over with a blank expression. He's hiding from me. Lucky him.

"Yes, sir," I whisper and go back to looking at the floor. A drop of blood splatters at my feet, soaking into the carpet. It's mine. I'm bleeding.

When a tear drips from my cheek and mingles with the crimson red droplets, I suck back a sob. I underestimated him. I forgot who he is, what he is.

Why won't he leave, why is he still standing in front of me? I chanced another glance, expecting to find a smug asshole glaring down at me.

"I'll be back," he says and heads for the door. "I expect you to eat everything on your dinner tray." He throws the dictate over his shoulder but doesn't even look at me. It's like he doesn't want to see me any more than I want to see him.

Once the door is closed and I'm alone again, my legs stop pretending to work and I sink to the floor. His cum is slipping out of me, mixed with my blood, but I don't care how messy it is.

The sobs come hard and fast now. No sense in trying to rein them in. Curling up with my knees pressed to my chest, I hug them and lean against the bed.

Accept my position, accept my situation.

KRISTOFF: BLAIRE'S WORLD

That's what he wants.
If this is my new life, I'd rather not have any at all.

7

Tricia ignores me as I stomp around the kitchen. She knows enough to back off when needed. And right now - it's needed.

"Where the fuck are all the apples?" I yell, slamming the refrigerator door. I like them cold. She knows this.

"We gave the last one to the new girl, this morning," she reminds me in her soft-spoken way. She's been under my father's control for too long; she doesn't even flinch when I slam my fist onto the counter near where she's working on chopping onions. Sometimes my father makes her cook for him. And since the usual kitchen staff isn't around, I assume he's put her on KP duty for the night.

I need a tray of food brought up to Magdalena, but I don't want to put that on

Tricia since it looks like my father has put her to work. Taking her away from the duties he gave her could end up with her strapped up on the wall and taking a caning from him.

"Where's Samantha?" I demand.

"She's been given to Matvei for the evening," Tricia says, but a drop of bitterness is laced in her tone. Not because she envies Samantha, but because she knows there's nothing she can do to stop it. If my father's given her to Matvei for the night, she'll be out of sight for a full day or two until she's able to move around enough to work.

I clench my teeth. "Why?"

She lifts a shoulder in a dainty shrug. "To make up for what you did to him." My father speaks freely in front of her, which works in my favor more times than not. But she doesn't glance at me when she tells me this news, knowing it won't make me happy. Giving that asshole a reward after I beat him down for touching what's mine doesn't exactly show my father backs my decisions.

"Fine. Get someone to help in here then. I need a tray of food brought up to my room. Pasta, something comforting - and a dessert." I drag my fingers through my hair. I need to get in a fucking shower.

Tricia stops chopping and looks sideways

at me. "Is there something else I can give her?" The question is quiet, and she knows asking is a risk.

I nod. "Yeah. Give her three ibuprofen tablets and a glass of wine - red." She'll still hurt, but at least it will buffer the pain. "And get the carpet cleaned up there too."

"Yes, sir." She goes back to chopping her onions.

I leave the kitchen, knowing Tricia will get it all done and head to my workout room. There's a full bathroom attached, and I can shower there without having to go back to my bedroom.

Because she's in there and I can't see her yet.

I can't look at that wounded look on her face. I turn the hot water on and step inside, dunking my head under the stream. Blood washes off my cock and pools at my feet before it swirls down the drain. Her blood.

"Fuck!" I yell into the shower.

Nothing with this girl has gone the way it's supposed to. I have a system. A very strict, easy system when I get a girl to train. I explain the situation. I set the rules. I show them what to expect and I teach them the shit they don't already know about serving a man sexually. But none of that has gone right with her.

I've fucked unwilling women before,

even harder than I fucked her, but I'd given them pleasure. They were high on orgasmic waves when I thrust my cock into them the first time.

This girl gets to me unlike any other I've trained. I haven't even started the training!

I need to get my head out of my ass and get the situation under control. She'll be pliable now. No more fighting me for control. Fuck, she doesn't even want control. This woman is a natural, willing submissive and all I have to do is tap into that - but instead she fights me every fucking step.

But right now, she's hurting. Not just from me forcing her, but she's starting to understand the hopelessness of her struggle. She can't win. She can't run. She'll just have to give in.

I turn off the water and dry off quickly. Right now, she's soft, if I work with her tonight, maybe she'll start to grasp the situation and work toward making the best of it. It doesn't have to be all bad. If she learns quick and does what she's told, I can get a good buyer for her. Someone who will at least take care of her - won't just stick her in a cell and fuck her whenever the mood strikes him.

Like my father does.

Just thinking of him makes my stomach

twist.

I grab a new pair of jeans, one without the stains of her blood on them, and yank them up.

After I finish dressing and comb back my wet hair, I make a call for the house physician to meet me at my apartment and head up to meet him. She'll be scared to see another man entering the room, it's best if I'm with him.

"Kristoff." Dr. Morrow nods in greeting when I find him at my door.

"Hey, doc." I shake his hand and snag the key from my pocket, letting us into the apartment. "She's in the bedroom." I consider going in first, to warn her about the exam - but disregard it. I can't coddle her, not now. She's had a shit day, and she needs to learn that shit days don't mean you don't have to follow rules and can decide what happens next. Going easy on her will only make things harder for her once she's transported at the end of the week.

If the good doctor has any concerns about the bedroom being dead-bolted from the outside, he's smart enough to keep them to himself. But he's been the physician at my father's estate for long enough to find very little about what goes on around here unusual.

Magdalena is sitting on the bed, blood

stains her thighs and the bedding beneath her. She hasn't washed, and by the look of the tray sitting on the end of the bed, she hasn't eaten either.

"Magdalena." I walk over to the bed. She doesn't react. "Magdalena," I say with more force. She looks up from her lap, streaks of dried tears stain her cheeks. Her eyes are bloodshot and puffy. "Magdalena, you were supposed to shower," I remind her but soften my voice.

"I—" she blinks. "I'm sorry." She unfolds her legs and scoots to the end of the bed. I help her stand and she gives me a wary look. She's scared. I feel it in her trembling body. She's frightened of me.

The dark pit in my stomach burns.

"Here, I'll help you, then the doctor can look you over. Okay?" I scoop her up into my arms and carry her to the bathroom.

She's stiff in my arms, doesn't answer me or fight me. Like a sack of flour.

"Warm bath should help," Dr. Morrow says as we pass him. "I'll strip the bed and call for Tricia to come change the sheets."

"She should have fucking done that when the food was brought up. I want to know why she didn't tell me this was going on." I nod toward my girl in my arms.

My girl.

Dangerous thinking for a man like me.

She can't be mine.

Especially not after what I've done.

I've broken her.

"I need you to sit here, okay?" I place her on the toilet lid and wait for her nod before I work on getting the tub filled with warm water. She won't look at me. She isn't crying anymore, but she won't speak either.

"Magdalena, did you take the ibuprofen I had sent up?" I ask, testing the water with my hand.

She nods.

"All three?"

She nods again.

"Why didn't you eat?"

A shrug.

"I told you to eat." I firm up my voice and at least I get a reaction. Her shoulders tense. "Let's get you cleaned up, then Dr. Morrow will check you over, and then you'll eat. Every damn bite. Understand?"

"Yes, sir," she whispers as though I hit the response button on her motherboard.

A fucking robot.

I sigh and lift her from where I have her perched and ease her into the bath. She leans back and closes her eyes, not stopping me in my mission of washing away all the evidence of the violence of our last encounter.

Other than tensing when I bring the

washcloth close to her pussy, she lets me have my way. For once. I shake my head, this isn't the submission I want from her.

"Do you hurt anywhere?" I ask, pulling apart her pussy lips and running the cloth gently through her folds.

"No," she lies. I glance at her and find a glimmer of fierceness in her eyes. The light isn't dead, just dimmed.

I don't chastise her for the lie, chasing her away now would be stupid. And I've already used up all my stupid for the day.

"Okay, lean your head back." I go about washing her hair. Short dark locks that easily allow my fingers to comb through. While she has her head leaned back, I admire her neck. Long and soft - a perfect place to kiss, to bite, to wrap my hand around.

"All done," I announce, and she pulls her knees up to her chest.

I uncork the tub and the glugging sound of the drain fills the space between us. I grab a towel from the rack. "Stand up."

She still doesn't move. I coddled too much.

"Now, Magdalena. I can't dry you off if you're sitting - get up." I hold out the towel. She grimaces with her movements but gets to her feet. "Hands at your sides," I order, and she listens.

I wouldn't mind a bit of snark at this moment.

"The doctor's waiting. And I expect you to do everything he says, no matter how you feel about it. Understand?" I finish wringing out her hair and point to the door.

"Yes, sir."

I'm beginning to hate that phrase.

"Good." I snap my fingers and move ahead of her, making her follow me into the bedroom. Tricia must have come and gone. The bed is remade. The tray has been moved to a nearby table.

"Hello, Magdalena." Dr. Morrow steps between us, blocking me from her view. "I'm Dr. Morrow. I work for the Dowidoff family and my job is to make sure you're in good health. I need you to lay on the bed for me, please. All right?" His pleasant voice grates on me. Her visual acceptance of him being there, her nod, irritates me more.

Dr. Morrow glances at me, then at a chair in the corner of the room. Obviously, he'd like me to stay out of his way.

No way.

I grab the chair and drag it to the side of the bed, within arm's reach of Magdalena. She could fight him and need to be restrained, I tell myself.

I'm a liar.

"How old are you, Magdalena?" Dr.

Morrow asks while snapping on a pair of gloves.

"Twenty-five," she answers softly. She seems younger to me, I would have thought twenty-one.

"Hmmm, and your last period, when was that?" He places the stethoscope to her chest.

"I have an IUD. I don't get my period anymore." Her eyes dart to me but refocus on the doctor quickly. At least we can be sure she didn't get pregnant.

"And your last sexual encounter?" He picks up her wrist and glances at his watch.

"A year ago," she says and turns her face away. "Other than today," she adds with a sour tone.

"If you weren't sexually active why do you have the birth control implant?" I ask, gaining a disapproving glare from Morrow.

She turns back with a hard glare. "I had horrible periods. Lots of blood. Lots of pain. Kind of like today." She swallows, and the fear returns to her expression. She's stepped on that line and she's not sure if I'm going to retaliate or not.

"I'm going to need to examine your vaginal area, Magdalena. Please drop your knees to the side, dear." Dr. Morrow ignores the little battle between us and leans over her. He's blocking my view of what he's doing, and I'm positive he's doing it on purpose.

He may work for our family, but that doesn't mean he's as big of an asshole as the rest of us. My father pays him too much to get in the way of our business with the girls he treats, but he still makes it his mission to treat the girls with a kindness I can't.

It's too dangerous to give them that. They won't have it when they leave us.

"No tearing. That's good." He pats her inner thigh and smiles up at her. "I need to check your backside, too, Magdalena, all right?" He asks her like she's allowed to deny or allow anything anymore.

She doesn't answer him but gives a small nod and rolls to her side. Dr. Morrow pulls her ass cheek up, spreading open the crevice where he'll find the tight hole I violated only hours ago.

I should look away, give her some sense of dignity, but I can't. I need to see what I've done, how much damage there is. The ring of muscle is still holding tight, but there's a tear. Even I can see it. A trickle of blood is still flowing.

Dr. Morrow shakes his head when he touches her, and she flinches but keeps his opinion about it to himself. Smart man.

"I don't think you'll need stitches here, but you will be very sore for a few days."

He releases her cheek and pats her hip, telling her he's all finished. He pulls off his gloves and turns to me, gesturing for me to follow him away from the bed and to the other end of the room. We won't be overheard.

Magdalena stays on her side, pulling her knees up to her chest again. I can see her bare ass, and the bruises from the belting turning a dark purple.

Dr. Morrow sees them too and frowns momentarily.

"She's fine. No permanent damage, but I wouldn't suggest any further use of her today, maybe not tomorrow either." He says this knowing I can't wait that long, she can't be given too much of a reprieve - she won't get any in the future with her new owner. "Stay away from her ass for as long as you can. She doesn't need to be stitched, but any further tearing could have bad results," he warns.

"Thanks." I nod, not commenting on his recommendations. Better he not know what's coming her way. Maybe he can sleep better at night that way.

Dr. Morrow nods, gathers his things, and whispers his goodbye to Magdalena. It's tempting to stop him and demand to know what he said, but she smiled softly after his words - so whatever it was, I'll let her keep them to herself.

After the doctor leaves and I rebolt the door, I walk over to the table with her dinner still on it.

"It's time to eat, Magdalena."

8

If Kristoff thinks giving me a bath and having a doctor check me out to be sure he didn't tear me in two, is going to make any of this better - he's more delusional than I had him pegged.

When I was a little girl, my mother would go in rampages over the dumbest things. She couldn't find her keys, she tripped over one of our shoes - everyday shit that happens to everyone. But she'd rage and scream and throw things and call us horrible names, and when she calmed down, she'd apologize. Give us ice cream for dinner or let us stay up past bedtime to watch a movie with her. None of it made me feel any better. But it probably took away some of her guilt.

Which is probably what Kristoff is doing - trying to wipe away his guilt. But that's his problem.

My problem is getting myself to snap out of this funk. I can't give up. I can't, but I'm too tired to fight him. I'm too scared of what's coming next. I hadn't thought he'd be capable of what he did.

What sort of things will the next man do?

"I'm not hungry, and it's probably cold," I say, still balled up on the bed. I should get under the covers, not let him see me naked - but it's not like he can't just rip them off me if he wants to get to my body again.

The pills he gave me have taken the edge off the pain, but I'm still sore in places I doubt ibuprofen can fix.

"Well, if it's cold that's your fault. And I don't care if you're hungry." He sits on the bed, putting the tray down in front of me and taking off the lids. A bowl full of pasta and veggies and a large piece of chocolate cake greets me. My stomach growls at the sight, and my mouth waters.

Pasta is my best friend in the world.

He'll just force me if I don't eat, so I scoot up to sit and crisscross my legs. The movements make the pain in my ass and shoulder spark to life, but I keep it to myself. He's been given enough of my pain for one day, he can't have anymore.

My hand is pushed away when I reach for the fork, and he grabs it.

"I don't need you to feed me, I'll eat," I say, but he's already loaded up the fork with pasta and a big chunk of tomato.

"You don't have a boyfriend back home? You said you haven't had sex in a year," he says and shovels the food into my mouth. I close my eyes at the deliciousness of the meal. Whoever made this dish, knew exactly what they were doing.

"Would it have changed anything if I do?" I ask after I swallow.

He pauses, gathers up some cake on the fork and brings it back to my lips. "Probably not."

At least he doesn't lie to me.

"How does a pretty girl like you not have a boyfriend or at least a few one-nighters in the past year?" he asks with a little tilt to his lips.

"How does a man kidnap, rape, and sell women, sleep at night?" I counter the question, feeling a bit braver since he's being civil. The monster who left my room hours earlier didn't return, but that didn't mean he wasn't still there. Lurking beneath the surface.

"Soundly," he deadpans. I can't tell if he's being sarcastic or serious, and it doesn't matter.

He hands me the fork and lets me scoop up more pasta.

KRISTOFF: BLAIRE'S WORLD

"Why are you investigating my father? You know how dangerous he is," he asks me, sounding more curious than demanding.

I shrug. "I've heard my sister talk about him. About what you do. I thought it would be a groundbreaking article."

"Sex trafficking?" he huffed a laugh. "It's not new, this thing he does," he says, and his accent thickens.

"No. But - he lives right here in England. Just like a normal person, and I wanted to see it. I was just going to snap some photos of the estate - from outside. Maybe talk to a few locals that know him." There's no reason to be telling him this, but he's got his feet propped up on the bed now, his hands folded behind his head. He's never looked so casual.

"And what about everything that happens inside?" he asks with darkened eyes.

"I wasn't going to try to get inside, yet." My plans weren't as developed as maybe he and his father think.

"You don't plan so much, do you? Sort of fly by the seat of your pants through life?" There's a lightness to his tone - one I'm not used to from him. It's unsettling.

I finish the cake without answering him. He doesn't deserve an answer and I'm worn out. My lids are heavy, and my knees hurt. Pushing the tray away from me, I uncurl my legs and shimmy under the covers.

His heavy sigh tells me he's getting annoyed again.

"Tomorrow is going to be rough for you," he announces, standing up from the chair. "We start training." He picks up the tray with the empty dessert dish and half-eaten pasta. "Get some sleep."

"Is training worse than what you did this afternoon?" I ask. A full stomach apparently has gotten rid of enough fear that I'm risking another beating - or worse.

His body stiffens when I mention our last encounter. The plates dance on the tray as he grips it tighter.

"Since you're less experienced than I thought, you have more to learn than I thought. We'll start discussing what experience you have as a submissive, then move onto other things."

My eyes widen.

He knows.

"Just because I didn't fuck everything that moved in the last year doesn't mean I'm inexperienced." I throw at him, the irritation in me not stopping my brain from firing at him. Am I really defending my sexual life to him?

"You'll have your chance to show me how much experience you have tomorrow," he says and leaves me alone once again.

Staring up at the ceiling, I run through the events of the day, the loss of hope, the pain. Everything he's been telling me is true.

I have no way out of this if my sister doesn't get to me in time. I still believe she will. She'll know something's wrong when I don't call her. I call her almost daily. When she doesn't get a text or call, she'll try to get a hold of me. She'll find me.

She's a fucking CIA agent! She'll find me.

It's my only option now.

9

Magdalena eats her entire breakfast without any warnings from me. Her eyes are a bit brighter in the morning sunlight, but I can still see the lingering fear from yesterday.

As much as it sours my stomach, it's better for her to have it. She should hold on to it, cradle it, because the fear will keep her obedient, and it will keep her safe.

From men like me.

No. From men worse than me.

"Stand up," I order and remove her empty plate from in front of her. Her hair is messy from sleep; she tossed and turned most of the night until I finally scooted over to her and wrapped my arm around her middle. Hugging her tightly to my body, she finally settled into a deep sleep and melted into me. Though I'm sure she doesn't recall any of this.

I shove the table to the wall and pull away her chair once she's on her feet.

"Move down to your knees, place your hands on your thighs palms down," I instruct her and wait for the resistance.

With as much grace as any woman I've trained before, she moves down to her knees, parts them and palms her thighs. She's not new to this.

"How long have you been submissive?" I ask, catching us both off guard. I'm curious, but it really has no bearing on what I planned for the day.

She glances up at me through her lashes and a soft pink hue tints her cheeks.

"Since my first boyfriend, I was seventeen." I'm more surprised by her answer than by my asking the question.

"A seventeen-year-old was a dominant?" I know it's possible. I trained my first slave for my father at eighteen, but I need to know more about her. She gives more freely when trying to contradict me.

"He wasn't seventeen." She looks back at her lap like she doesn't want to tell me the rest of it. Which means I need to know.

"How old was he?" I ask with a sigh. I really don't like dragging answers from people.

"Twenty-two." The blush on her cheeks deepen, and her fingers are digging into her thighs.

I reach down to cup her chin and pull her gaze back to me. Hiding doesn't work for me, and she really should know that by now.

"Is he the man who took your virginity?" My question has nothing to do with the training we're going to begin, but I want to know. I feel a burning need to know as much about Magdalena as I can.

"No, well - we didn't have sex, just - well, other things." Talking about this is making her blush. She has a modest tinge to her soul. I like it.

"How did you date a man five years older than you and come away still a virgin?" It seems unlikely. If she was half as fuckable at seventeen as she is now, the man must have been cockless.

"Unlike you - he respected women. He didn't go further than I wanted him to." She spits the answer at me with a venom in her tone that scalds me. This girl knows exactly which buttons to press.

"A twenty-two-year-old trying to get into the pants of a seventeen-year-old isn't a man who respects women. He's a man chasing tail and saying whatever he needs to get it. I bet you dated for two months, maybe three.

He wouldn't wait longer than that. He spanked you a little, maybe did some bedroom bondage with his ties? Then he realized the gates were sealed shut on that pretty pussy of yours, and he hightailed it out." Her eyes widen more with every word I say, and I want to find this asshole and put my fist through his face.

"It- it wasn't like that. He took a new job and needed to relocate." She says it like she's convincing herself I'm wrong. Except I'm never wrong. Not when it comes to men's intentions.

"Hmmm." I release her chin, noting my finger marks linger on her creamy skin before slowly fading away.

"It wasn't," she whispers to her lap.

"You've played then, with other men?" I go back to the insane line of questioning I began. It really doesn't matter how much experience she's had with impact play, or blood play, or anything else. Whatever her owner wants to do to her she'll endure - because she won't have a choice. There won't be a safeword for her to cry out when it's too much. And it will be too much.

I unclench my fists and take a step away from her. I need space, I need to remember that she's not mine to protect. She can't be. She's mine to train, that's it.

"Yes, mostly casual. Nothing serious."

She flicks her hair back over her shoulder.

"No more boyfriends?"

She shakes her head. "None that were serious."

"Sexual experience? Other than actual sex. Have you sucked a cock before?" Just the idea of her sweet lips wrapped around my cock has it standing at attention. "I know you've had your pussy eaten - at least once." I grin, remembering how easily she melted into my hands when I took her clit in my mouth. Fuck she tasted good. I won't wait too much longer before having another serving.

"Yes. I've done that. I just told you I did other things," she answers with her teeth gritted. I wonder if I touch her will her pussy be wet for me. Her pupils are already dilated, and her breathing is a bit shallower.

I clear my throat. "Good."

"I don't want this. You understand that, right? It's wrong, what you're doing. What your father does. It's wrong." Her voice is firm but low. If she's trying to tap into my conscience, she's wasting her time.

"So is child labor, forced work camps, poor health care, homelessness, child abuse, the list goes on." I fist her hair and pull her head back, mostly because I like to see her in that position, on her knees, looking up at me with her neck elongated and waiting for me to lick it. Or better yet, bite it.

"That's not—"

"There will always be bad things, bad people in the world, Magdalena. You will not change this."

Her jaw clenches. "Maybe not, but Danuta can." The conviction in her words almost has me convinced. Almost.

I force a laugh. "I don't think you know your sister as well as you think you do."

"She's my sister. Of course, I do," she protests, and I tighten my hold on her hair, enjoying the wince of pain cross her face.

"No. Magdalena. My innocent girl, you know very little about so many things." I pat her cheek and release her. "Now, press your cheek to the floor and wait for me to step up to you. When I do, kiss my boot gently with your lips and wait for me to release you. This is how you'll greet your new owner after the sale is finished."

"I can't." She shakes her head.

"There is no room for ego when you become a slave to these men. They will not hesitate to hurt you."

Her dark eyes meet mine. Resistance lingers there.

"Magdalena, I'm trying to make this easier on you. If you know what to do, what to expect, things will go better." I almost laugh at my words. I know what I'm doing, and what I'm forcing her into. She's not the first slave to be trained in my apartment, but she's the first that makes me question it. She's not just another sale. She's become something more. Something I don't deserve.

The nod is slow in coming, and when it does, she closes her eyes. Defeated again. My victories don't taste as sweet with her. They are tainted sour by the pain she tries to mask from me - unsuccessfully.

She shifts her hands to the floor, sliding them out in front of her and presses her right cheek to the rug.

"Danuta will come," she whispers to herself. No one's coming for her, but I won't break her thin veil of hope.

I step around her, looking at the bruises on her back and what I can see of her ass. Needing a better look, I hook my boot under her pussy and push her ass up in the air. She grumbles but doesn't try to stop me. When I remove my boot, I see her juices have coated the tip.

The bruises are fine. Ugly and dark in a few spots, but they'll fade enough for the auction in a few days. Stepping back around, I place my boot in front of her.

"After you've greeted me, lick off the mess your pussy made," I instruct, folding my hands in front of me. I'm aware her body is reacting to the situation on autopilot and her mind hasn't caught up to it, but the motions will eventually get her there.

She lifts and turns her head, leaning forward with her lips puckered already. Softly she presses her lips to the worn black leather of my boot.

"Clean it, Magdalena. That pretty pussy of yours is soaked with desire."

Her little pink tongue slips out from between her plump lips and laps up the bit of juice not already dried. She takes long licks and leans farther into my boot, rising her ass farther in the air.

She's not hating this.

"That's a good girl," I praise her when she moves back into position, her cheek once again pressed to the floor.

Squatting down, I brush her hair from her face, so I can see her more clearly. Her cheeks are flushed again. No, she didn't hate it.

"You've been very good this morning, my girl." I switch to my own language, knowing she understands me. There's a smile tugging at her lips, but she fights against it. Running the back of my hand along her jawline, I watch her internal struggle in silence. "I'm going to reward you."

Her legs, which were still parted, snap together and I laugh. "None of that now. If I want to touch you there, you know I will."

Tension seizes her body. She's afraid I'll force her again. I may have eased some of the terror from her with caring for her yesterday afternoon, but I haven't erased the act. Nothing I do will ever remove it from her memory. It will haunt her nightmares forever if she lets it. And it's my fault - I put the horror there.

"I have a treat for you." I leave her where she is and go to my closet. When I return, her eyes are closed, and her eyelashes are wet. She's trying her best not to cry but failing.

"Kneel up." I don't comment on the tears. Those are hers to keep. "A vibrator," I announce sounding stupidly like some kid at show and tell. Clearing my throat, I hold it out for her.

She takes the U-shaped toy from me and looks it over. It's shaped perfectly to fit around her body, to stimulate her clit all the way to her asshole.

I squat down and pluck it from her, showing her how it works. "It cups your body," I say and point out the switch. "There's where it gets turned on."

When she remains silent, I reach down between her legs and get the toy situated for her. She jerks when the thin elongated edge snuggles between her ass cheeks, but she doesn't try to move out of my reach. I know she's still sore there, but I also know a little bite of pain will help her.

Once it's in place, I run my hand up her body, over her taut stomach, and over her breasts. Her nipples harden beneath my touch, and I take my time rolling them between my fingers and massaging her tits. Her body responds to my touch like it understands she owns nothing at the moment, but it's her mind I want. I want her full submission.

She's watching my face as I fondle her, like she's trying to figure me out. Good luck.

"You're going to ride my boot with the vibrator on. It will help give more friction, you'll see - and you'll like it."

She huffs. "I won't like anything you do to me."

I let my lips curl in a slow smile. "Little liar. You're also going to wrap these pretty lips." I pause to run my thumb over her bottom lip. "Around my cock until I come down your throat."

Again, she freezes. "And if I don't want to - you'll force me." Those damn tears. They seem to irritate her as much as me though, and she swipes them away with the back of her hand.

"No." I wipe away a missed tear running

down her cheek. "No more forcing." It's a promise I've never made before, but I'll keep it. I won't force her. There are other ways to gain her cooperation, other methods that bring pleasure to us both.

"But defiance will be punished, Magdalena." Another promise, not any less true than the first.

She blinks, and her throat works as she swallows. A snarky response is rolling around that pretty head of hers, but she's learned enough to keep it from rolling off her tongue.

I slide my foot closer to her and grab her hair, yanking her forward until she positions herself on me. Lifting my toes up, I reach down and flick the switch on the vibrator.

Her moan is almost instant.

10

I have to stop reacting to him. But the vibrations run over my clit at the perfect speed and when he lifts his foot again, it presses down hard. The friction - oh fuck the friction. And the vibrations are moving through the whole device, over my entrance, and over my ass.

"There - see, good girl." He's speaking in Russian. With his free hand, he unbuckles his belt and pulls his zipper down. His cock bobs, smacking me in the mouth. He groans, like the sight of it turns him on.

I won't blame him for it, this time.

He said he wouldn't force me. I look at his thick cock in front of me and play with the idea of denying him. Testing his word. Except he wiggles his foot and another round of intense sensations rock my body.

"Open that pretty mouth of yours," he says in his hard voice. The authority is there, underlining his demand and I obey. Like the good girl he calls me, I part my lips wide and stick out my tongue. "So good." He growls and fists the base of his cock, aiming it at my mouth.

It's big and I have to readjust my lips to accommodate him as he edges his way in my mouth. When the head of his cock touches my throat, I swallow, working hard to keep from gagging, but he pushes too hard too fast and I start to sputter. He pulls back, not enough to leave me, but enough for me to get much-needed air.

"Again," he says and yanks me by my hair down his shaft. Again, I swallow and manage better this time. I run my tongue over his hard length, tasting him and wanting more of it. I go farther down, taking him until his dark curls at the base tickle my nose. It takes concentration to do this and I've almost forgotten the vibrator on my sex.

But he won't let me forget, and he wiggles his damn foot again. I lose my composure and moan at the pleasure working its way over my pussy, making me even wetter. His boot will be covered again by the time we're finished. Having moved my focus, I have to pull back on his cock, but he won't let me and shoves himself down my throat.

I cough and gag, but he won't let me up.

"Take it like a good girl, Magdalena. Swallow my cock," he orders, but it sounds like he's gritting his teeth. Is he on the edge, too?

Spit pools at the corners of my mouth. When he finally pulls back, I gasp for much-needed air and the saliva pours out of my mouth, down my chin, over my chest. Before I fully recover, he yanks my head back again and thrusts into my mouth. I'm ready this time and swallow immediately.

"Open wide," he says and moves his hand from my hair to hook his thumbs inside my mouth. I open as big as I can. The force of his cock fucking my mouth unsteadies me and I balance myself with my hands pressing against his thighs. Such fucking masculine thighs.

I inhale through my nose, taking in his scent, basking in the muskiness of it.

He readjusts his stance and his foot grinds into my clit. I moan, rolling my eyes. The vibrations are overtaking my senses. My stomach swirls with pressure. I'm going to explode.

"Good girl, fuck yourself with my boot," he says in English, his accent thick. My hips are moving, I'm fucking myself with his boot, I'm being a good little obedient slut for him. But I can't care about it now.

I'm hungry.

I'm starved.

For his cock.

My release.

My eyes snap open as the ripples of pleasure burst into an explosion that sucks the air from my lungs. I can't help but scream and ride his boot harder, faster, chasing after every orgasmic flutter.

Kristoff thrusts with more power into my throat and I give a muffled cry.

"Fuck, baby, yes." He grunts and yanks my face down his length. I sputter but manage to keep him snug as hot streams of his cum spurt down my throat. I swallow it as it comes, but my body is starting to soften, the high from my orgasm is crashing and I grip his thighs, trying to push him away.

"All. Of. It." He growls. I swallow, but there's too much, and he's still moving inside my mouth. When he's done, when he's caught his breath, he releases my lips and I pull back. His seed is running down my chin, and I wipe it away.

"I said all of it, Magdalena," he reminds me between his quick breaths and bends over and grabs my hand, forcing it to my mouth.

My lips burn from his treatment, and I

can barely catch air for myself, but he's not letting go. When has he ever not gotten his way in this room?

I stare at the string of cum smudged over the back of my hand and begin to lick it clean.

"So much better today," he praises me after dropping my hand and pets my head.

"Asshole," I mutter and start to get to my feet after removing the vibrator.

"I didn't say to stand. You remain on your knees until you're given permission to use your feet. And you'd better practice on muttering more quietly. If your owner hears you insult him, he'll be quick to punish."

I get back down and glare up at him. "And you? Will you punish me?" A part of me wishes he would. I deserve it for enjoying what he just fucking did. I shouldn't have gotten any satisfaction from sucking his cock, and I sure as fuck shouldn't have wiggled around on his boot like his personal whore and came so damn hard. No. I deserve a solid whipping. Maybe it would knock the sense back into my head.

"Always." He nods and begins to lace the leather of his belt back through the buckle. "But in this case, it's true. I am an asshole. The other men - they are worse but don't admit it. I'm fully aware of what and who I am." A hint of sadness, dark resolve, taints his powerful voice. "But if you say it again, I will make you scream for mercy from the number of orgasms I will give you."

I clamp my mouth closed. I've had orgasms forced on me before. Date a sadist, and it's one of the things you'll get. Not my favorite afternoon activity. And I doubt Kristoff will stop after an easy number like three.

"You may get up and wash up. I have meetings this afternoon, but Stephania will be up in a bit with lunch, and to work on your hair." His belt is buckled, and he yanks up his zipper. The sound draws my attention, but I realize quickly I'm staring at his groin.

Fuck.

He's grinning like a loon when I glance back up at him.

"What's wrong with my hair?" I demand. Other than it being all messed up from his continual attacks at grabbing it.

"Nothing. But she's going to be getting you ready for the auction in a few days, and it's easier if she has an idea of what she's working with. You'll be nice to her, and you won't bother her with any questions or try to get her to help you. She's worked with my father for over a decade. She's loyal to him and trying to get her to side with you will only get your ass in trouble."

"Fine." If she's anything like Tricia, asking her anything would be a waste of breath anyway.

He shakes his head and heaves a heavy sigh. "You'll end up black and blue if you keep this up." He steps toward me, and I flinch when he grabs my arm. Spinning me around, he whacks my ass half a dozen times before it even registers that he's spanking me. I hop from one foot to the other and try to cover my ass, but he simply avoids my hands.

"Watch your tone and mind your words!" He punctuates each word with a strong pop. By the time he's finished, I'm out of breath and weak. I've never had trouble remembering to use the word Sir before, but it's different here. It doesn't fit him. But my burning ass reminds me I need to say it, if only for the sake of being able to sit.

I'm spun around again, and he presses his forehead to mine. For a moment, I'm sure he's going to kiss me; he wraps his hand around my neck holding me to him. But he makes a growling sound and shoves me away from him.

"She'll be up soon," he says and marches out of the room. My ass hurts from the short spanking, but I don't bother trying to rub away the sting. I just add the ache to the rest of them.

KRISTOFF: BLAIRE'S WORLD

What the hell is taking my sister so long? She has to have realized I'm missing by now, and surely, she can figure out where I am.

I only have four more days left by my calculations. If she doesn't get me, if I don't find a way out of this place, I could really become property to someone much meaner than Kristoff. Someone that would love to see me in pain and bleed for them. I've heard horrible stories, seen pictures of the victims once they are found after being discarded.

I can't become one of them.

11

Andrei has called for me, interrupting my plans to bring up a book for Magdalena to read. Being kept in one room for days on end starts to play with the mind, and I need her to be sharp when it comes time to sell her at auction. A broken slave is seen as a whipping post, and I can't have her fall into the hands of some bastard who gets off on slicing and dicing his women.

I hand off the book to one of the servants with the new security code to my apartment and instructions to make sure Magdalena gets the material. It's just an old novel I found in the library. My father doesn't read, no one on the compound uses the damn room other than to hold meetings and look smarter than they actually are.

"Kristoff!" my father greets me when I

walk into his office. He's puffing on a thick cigar and walking to his desk. "I thought you'd be busy with your little pet." He flashes me a grin I know too well. The forced sort that sends the hairs on my neck stand at attention. He's not pleased.

"You needed something?" I ask, not taking the bait. So that's his problem. He doesn't like that I've moved Magdalena from the cells downstairs to my apartment.

The corners of his lips fall, morphing his grin into a mild sneer.

"Yes. I've been given an offer for the girl." He stands behind his desk. I won't sit until he does, he knows this and keeps standing.

"You said you would auction her off," I remind him, my mind already playing out scenarios of what monster has put a bid in early.

"Yes, but this offer is too large to give up. Maksim wants her. He's offered double his last purchase. We won't see that profit at an auction," he explains, puffing again on his cigar. He's right. Twice the amount would cover the purchase of two or three girls.

"Why does he want her so badly? He has his own stock of women, his own slaves." The stories I've heard of the women he keeps makes my stomach turn. Has he grown tired torturing his own women and now wants fresh meat?

Andrei's eyebrows kick up in curiosity. I've never asked about a buyer before. I realize my mistake too late to take it back. Though I'm sure he's already having his own theories.

"Why do you care?" he asks, pointing the cigar at me. "That's what I want to know. You stop Matvei from having some fun with the new toy, and then you lock her away in your apartment? What's going on, Kristoff?"

My hands clench at my sides, but I force them back open, softening my stance. He can't see what I'm feeling. Over the years I've gotten very good at hiding my distaste for him, my repulsion at the man he is - I can't let him see it now.

"It's not like Maksim, that's all." I fold my arms over my chest. "When will he make the pickup, or should I get a transport ready." Saying the words nearly strangle me.

"I haven't decided if I'm going to take the offer. Maksim - he pisses me off with his attitude and disrespect. Like he's so high up the food chain no one can touch him." Him telling me about the offer is his way of seeing my reaction, seeing if I'll protest it, but I haven't gotten that far into thinking about it. He just gave me a ray of hope.

"I'll keep to the schedule then until you

decide." I drop my hands and turn to leave. Waste of fucking time, this talk. His games are easily seen through. Maksim is a bigger player because he uses his fucking head for business. He's grown his business, he's spread out past just trafficking. My father can't keep his dick clear of pussy long enough to think past trying out his newest slave.

"I need you tonight." His words stop me just as I reach for the handle. His voice, deeper, darker than usual. "There's a meeting I need you to take care of for me. A new buyer is in town for the night, wants some ass kissing. You're going to take care of it for me. It will be good practice for you for when you take over the business."

He says this like he's handing over a grocery list.

"Don't worry about your pet. I'll make sure she's put through her paces tonight." I can't help the acid feeling in my stomach, it's churning and twisting in my stomach, burning a hole through me. To tell him no would set him off.

"You want her tonight?" I ask, trying to sound merely curious. He doesn't usually get involved until the women are ready for auction. No patience for unpolished toys, and he can't afford to mark the product before it goes on the auction block.

"Yes." He nods and rolls his wrist. "It's been awhile since I worked with a new toy."

I step toward him but catch myself before I lose myself. I've done too much to move forward to let him piss me off and shove me back.

"Don't worry. Dr. Morrow told me - her ass is off limits for a bit longer. I won't touch her there." His promise knocks the breath from me, but I recover quickly. He's been talking to the doctor. He knows what happened, what condition her body is in.

"What time is the dinner?" I ask, changing the topic. Even if I find a way out of going to the meeting, I can't deny him access to her. To do so would make things worse for her, because Andrei doesn't need an excuse to take things to the next level. And any sort of resistance on my end would push him in that direction.

"Seven-thirty. It's in London so you'll need to leave soon. I'll have a car ready for you." His smile doesn't reach his eyes. But any sort of decent life had flickered out of them years ago. Nothing but a shell of a human remained. The parts that desired power and money and didn't give a fuck on how he got either.

But was I so different?

"Fine. I'll get ready."

"I've had the girl brought to my room

already," he tells me when I've opened the door. I grit my teeth and give a curt nod.

I won't have a chance to warn her, to beg her to behave. She's going to have to get through this on her own.

Heading up to my room, I have to hold onto the hope that she's learned something in the past few days. That maybe she will heed my warnings.

Holding onto hope. Sounds more like her thing than mine. Maybe I'm learning a few things from her, too.

KRISTOFF: BLAIRE'S WORLD

12

A strangling stench wakes me. Burning fills my lungs and I gasp for air while coughing out the fumes tinging my insides. An attempt to lift my hands fail.

Frantically, I yank and pull, but my wrists are bound in front of me. When I open my eyes, I'm still shrouded in darkness. My feet are as useless as my hands. Where am I?

Reminding myself to keep calm doesn't help much, but I force my memory to search for the truth. What the fuck happened?

I had been standing near the windows in Kristoff's room. Not bothering with the idea of escaping through them anymore once I had seen the distance to the ground below. The door to his room had burst open, startling me, and men charged me.

Yanking harder on the binds on my

wrists, I survey my position. I'm bent over, knees on cushioned planks and my hands bound below my chest. A spanking bench? I've been in this particular contraption before, though my legs are spread much wider than I remember. My ass is propped up with a pillow, or a leather wedge. I can't fucking tell because there's a damn blindfold over my eyes.

"Ah, good. You are finally awake." Andrei's thick accent sends a sharp shiver down my spine. The room's cold, but his presence chills me further. Where is Kristoff?

"What do you want?" I demand, turning in the direction I think he's standing. There's a slight echo after I speak. I don't think I'm in the comfort of Kristoff's apartment anymore. At the realization, the dampness of the room settles into my skin. I'm back in the lower levels of the house - where the cells are.

He laughs. "I already have what I want."

Being obtuse isn't helping my level of anxiety. I'm naked, bound, and in prime position for things I've read about in news articles and police reports. I yank harder, pull with more force on my ankles. His laughter bounces off the walls and I hear more shuffling.

"Where's Kristoff?" I ask, simmering

down. There are more people here now, I can feel them. I sense their fucking erections.

"My son is busy." His tone sours with his statement. There's more between Andrei and Kristoff than just being father and son. And as curious as I am about that, right now I need to figure out how to get the fuck off the spanking bench and back into Kristoff's room.

"Then—"

He scoffs and slaps me hard across my face, snapping my head to the side. "You talk too much," he reprimands me and grabs my hair, pulling my head back. I would probably be looking right into those dark beady little eyes of his, except he's taken away my sight with the damn blindfold.

"You're here as a gift. My men have been working hard and they deserve a little fun. My son has been too soft with you."

"Soft?" A little laugh comes out of me. Probably from the fear penetrating my body. I'm slowly piecing together what Andrei's words mean.

"I don't really care if you accept your position or if you don't. Most men I work with prefer you fight them. Same goes for tonight. However, I don't want my men's cocks bitten off, so you'll need to be restrained a bit more. Matvei? Come, put the ring in, then you and the other men may begin."

My hair's released, and I whip my head to one side then the other, I have to get away, I have to. There's no fucking way I'm letting anyone touch me.

Kristoff said there'd be no more forcing.

Kristoff's not here.

Why isn't he here? Why would he let his father take me?

My head is grasped between two strong hands and lifted up. The blindfold is eased away from my eyes, just above my brow. After blinking a few times, I see him. Matvei. From my cell when I first came. Kristoff saved me from him once.

The pit in my stomach warns me from hoping he'll do it again.

"Ahh, you remember me? Hmm? Good." He pats my cheek then grips my chin, pulling my jaw downward. His other hand yanks my head back.

"Fuck you." I try to sound fierce. But the smile that reveals his yellowing teeth, tells me I only humor him.

"That's the plan," he says in Russian. I realize both of them had spoken Russian, and I've answered. Not that my language skills was much of a defense, but at least it gave me the chance to overhear them. They could speak more freely thinking I didn't understand.

"I won't let you," I say and clamp my teeth shut.

"You have no say, no choice. You are a whore, just a little plaything for me and my friends here." He looks up and away from me. "Come, come over and let her see you. Let her know how many cocks are going to be shoved into her cunt, her ass, and her mouth."

There's a little tilt to his lips. He's really having a good time. I might vomit.

Four men shuffle from behind me and line up behind him. All of them have their shirts off and their cocks hanging out of their jeans. They are stroking themselves, like ravenous wolves waiting for the feast to begin.

My struggles increase, but nothing's changed. I'm just as bound, just as naked.

"No ass," Andrei announces from somewhere in the room. "Kristoff did a thorough job of breaking her there, I don't want more damage. We only have a few days before the sale."

Matvei's smile falls, but he nods in agreement.

He releases me, and I drop my head. This isn't happening. Kristoff will burst in any minute. Or maybe my sister will find me. Now is the perfect time for a rescue mission.

Right now.

A steel ring is pressed to my lips, but I fight to keep it out. Turning my head, clamping my lips, but he's stronger. So much stronger.

I'm slapped again, this time stars burst into my vision and when I open my mouth to work the pain out of my jaw, the ring is shoved in. He easily maneuvers it to keep my mouth propped open and he buckles it behind me, tossing the blindfold from my head.

"Don't want you to miss a thing," he says with the cheer of a kid in a candy store and pats my head.

He stands up, unzips his jeans and pulls out his cock. If I wasn't about to piss myself at the idea of all these men touching me, I'd laugh. He's pencil-thin - long, but so thin I don't think he needed the ring in my mouth at all.

My hair is yanked again, and his cock shoves into my throat. I gag at the intrusion and fight to pull back, but he holds my head. In and out he fucks my throat. The width of his cock doesn't matter, he makes up for it in length. My throat stretches around him, but he's going too fast, and I can't breathe.

"Fuck yes." He growls over me and grabs both sides of my head, thrusting harder into me, faster. I sputter and cough around his dick, but he never relents. "Iosif, smack her ass! I want to see the jiggle while I fuck her whore mouth."

A second later a hard slap to my ass jolts me forward, making me take the cock farther down.

Matvei laughs. "Good. Again!" he calls and another smack, and another. Every time Iosif hits me, I'm jolted forward. Matvei is getting a show and a blow job.

Finally, he pulls out of my throat and I sputter more, clearing my throat and spitting onto the ground. I'll never get the taste of him out of my mouth.

Another smack hits my ass, but it's different. Iosif is standing in front of me. His hand is working over his cock, stroking it until a large bead of pre-cum sits on the edge. He steps over to me and rubs it on my cheek with a laugh.

While I'm trying to move my face away from him, Matvei thrusts his cock into my pussy. I scream at the intrusion. Pain ricochets through my body as he slaps me repeatedly and shoves his cock into me over and over again. The burn overwhelms me. His fingers dig into my hips as he fucks me. I struggle, wiggle, moving everything in my body that can move, but it does nothing. I'm completely helpless.

Why hasn't the door opened yet? This is

exactly when the hero is supposed to be charging in, but the door isn't opening.

Iosif shoves his cock into my mouth, stifling my scream when Matvei thrusts particularly hard.

"Viktor, Here, you fuck her next," Matvei says and yanks out of me. My mind doesn't have time to comprehend the dick being thrust down my throat, choking me because my cunt is burning again, stretching around a thick cock.

I'm yelling, screaming, but everything is muffled. Pain hits me from both ends of my body. The fucking ring keeps my mouth opened wide enough for Iosif to keep throat-fucking me with ease. Too much ease for him. I can't get enough air. When I try to use my tongue to push him out, he wraps a hand around my throat.

"Such a nice pussy," Viktor says from behind me. "So fucking tight." He smacks my ass with appreciation. "Good ass too! You sure we can't fuck it a little?" he asks, thrusting harder into me.

"No ass. Have fun with her." Andrei's voice carries over from somewhere and I hear the door.

Finally! Kristoff will help me. I'm expecting his roar of outrage, but instead I hear the steel door close.

"Take my cock," Iosif grunts, pulling my

ears toward him and shoves his dick all the way into my throat. I'm gagging hard, but he holds me there, the coarse curls of his pubic hair tickle my nose. "Oh, fuck." He growls, retreats then plunges forward.

Thick cum spurts down my throat. He's grunting his orgasm, and pulls back, letting more of the hot ropes of his release hit my tongue and then steps back and smacks my face with his cock. He's still coming and it's dripping on my cheeks and nose.

He grunts in satisfaction and steps away. "Fuck that's good."

"You asshole! You didn't even fuck her yet!" one of the other men jeer him.

Iosif laughs. "Her throat was fucking sweet."

"Let me in there, then." Viktor pulls out of my pussy and steps in around me.

I'm trying to catch my breath, trying to wrap my brain around what's happening. Because this can't be reality. This has to be a dream, and I need to wake up. I need to wake up right now.

Another cock is shoved into my pussy and I cry out. Too big. It's too fucking big. I scream when he pulls back and thrusts forward. I'm wet now, but it's not helping, it still stings. The stretch is unbearable.

"Come here, bitch." My hair is yanked and before I can see who has me, he shoves his own dick into my throat. Again, I sputter, but he's just as ruthless.

None of them care. I'm just a slab of meat laying here. A fuck toy.

My ass is slapped again, and another hand slips between my chest and the bench and twists my nipple.

A round of laughter erupts, but I can't tell where it's coming from. Another twist and another scream. It keeps going like this. I'm fucked hard from behind; sharp nails dig into my hips. When one thrusts, the other pulls back. My throat hurts, my back hurts from arching in an attempt to get away.

But I'm not going to get away.

I'm just a plaything now.

Not even human.

And no one is coming to save me.

This is my reality.

"Fuck, yes!" The man behind me, I've lost track of who it is, yanks out and his cum splashes all over my ass and back. "Fucking whore." He grunts as he finishes his orgasm.

I'm given no reprieve before the next dick is shoved in. Thicker, much thicker and I'm back to screaming around someone's shaft.

"Her throat is so fucking tight," I hear him say, and swallow, trying not to gag and suffocate on him. My chin is coated with saliva, it's dripping from me.

"Try her cunt. Oh fuck!" The man behind me pushes in, all the way. I can feel his balls slapping my pussy. Liquid runs down my thigh. Is he coming?

The burn of my throat distracts me from the stretch and sting from my pussy but only for a brief moment. I'm not left alone, and when I think I can maybe stand it, when I find a small corner of my mind to hide in until this is over, a burn like I've never felt before crosses my back.

"She marks beautifully," I hear just before another lash lands across my shoulder blades. I'm being whipped.

Tears pour down my cheeks, mingling with dried and fresh cum. The men are moving around me, shoving into my pussy, my mouth, pulling my hair, whipping my back and my ass.

Pain burst from every area of my body, and my mind isn't allowed to hide. Once again, my hair is pulled until I'm looking up at my offender. I can't see clearly enough through my tears, but it seems he's pleased. He's smiling. And after he spits on my face, in my mouth, he's laughing, and he shoves my head back down and forces his cock into my mouth.

My jaw aches from the ring, my tongue and mouth would be dry except more cum coats them when this man comes on me.

"I want her ass," I hear, and I stiffen. No. Andrei told them no. Didn't he?

"You'll be putting your cock on the line. Andrei won't tolerate it. Stick to her pussy." Another lash crosses my ass and I scream. Drool and cum drip off my chin, and I try to suck in as much air as I can before someone fills my throat again.

But my mouth is left alone. I'm fucked again. I don't cry out. I don't scream. I use the break for my throat and drop my head. Grunts and cheers surround me, but I'm far away now. I feel all of it, I feel the last bit of cum splashing over my ass and back, but I'm empty. All the fear all the hope - it's gone.

I'm just empty.

Completely empty.

13

Andrei is an asshole. I know this. I grew up learning this fact every day. I thought I knew his tricks, all of them. But he's up to something now.

The meeting wasn't what he said it would be. I have to see Magdalena.

My muscles are twisted with tension. The pounding in my head matches the horrible dance shit the men play when they party.

I need a drink.

Then I'll see Magdalena.

I spent the entire meeting worrying about her, wondering what my father was doing with her. My initial plans were to get the meeting over with and get my ass home to intervene if needed. But nothing has gone according to plan this week.

"Ah, Kristoff. You're home!" Andrei

steps into the main hallway. He's been waiting for me and is trying to play it off like he wasn't. The thunder in my head increases.

"Where's Magdalena?" I ask before stopping myself. He's holding a glass of vodka, an unlit cigar stuffed between his fat fingers. The look of satisfaction at my question answers it.

"I was just going to check on her, come." He crooks a finger and heads to the back of the house where his office is located.

Matvei passes us in the hall, a smirk crosses his lips when he nods at me and keeps walking. I turn to stare at him, but my father has called for me to keep moving.

My stomach is in knots. Something is very wrong.

"What did you do?" I ask with a dark undertone. It's getting harder to keep my composure after the evening I've had and the sense of dread starting to overwhelm me.

"Me? I did nothing," he says with a slight shrug of his shoulders. When we reach his office, he shuts the door behind me and makes his way to the television stashed in the corner of the room. He only uses it to tap into the security feeds in the cells downstairs.

Blood rushes from my head.

"But, the men - they needed to blow off

some steam." He picks up the remote to the television and flicks a button.

My father stands to the side of me, giving me a clear view of the screen.

Magdalena. Strapped down over a spanking bench. Her wrists and ankles bound, her eyes covered with a black rag. She's squirming on screen, but at least she's alone.

But then my father appears.

This is the past. This has already happened. My mouth dries.

The volume is off, so I can't hear what my father said to her, but more men show up. Five in total.

Somehow, I manage to keep my face blank, at least I hope I do. Andrei is checking for a response from me. I'm too busy memorizing the faces of the men I'm going to kill.

Matvei moves to stand in front of Magdalena and slaps her. My hands fist, but I don't speak. I watch in silence.

Andrei turns the volume on when Matvei shoves his pencil cock into her mouth. Her screams fill the room, but I still say nothing. I'm plotting. I'm planning. I'm trying not to experience this, but then force myself to.

She experienced it. She felt every thrust, every lash, every drop of their disgusting cum on her body. I've heard her cry out from the beltings I've given her, from my own savage use of her body, but these are different. These are strangled and horrific.

Her body is shaking by the time the third man starts toying with her. Angry welts cross her back and ass, traces of blood mingle with the semen coating her skin. Spit is falling from her open mouth and tears run from her cheek and mix with the mess on the floor below her. She vomited. The asshole didn't even stop fucking her face while she did. That man will die slower than the rest.

"She's a good fuck, the men tell me," my father says when I remain stoic, not taking my eyes off the screen. I don't deserve to hide from this act.

"Where is she now?" I ask when the last man finally tucks his cock, covered with her blood, back into his jeans.

"I had no more use for her, so I had her brought up to your room." My father downs his drink and places the glass down on a table.

I keep my eyes on the screen. The men leave her, and all that's left is her sobs. They removed the ring from her mouth, but she's not saying anything. She spits blood, and it covers her thighs as well.

The assholes have torn her.

"Did the meeting go well?" He changes

topics, but I'm not done with this one yet.

"You let those men touch my girl?" I ask in a low growl.

His expression darkens. "You mean my girl. She's mine, Kristoff. You forget yourself."

"What are you playing at?" I demand.

"You've become too attached to this one," he responds. "You will finish her training, and she will be delivered to Maksim next week."

My mind flips to his course of topic. "Maksim? You said you weren't decided about accepting his offer. He's an asshole, and what need does he have of another girl?" He's been playing me all night, like a fine-tuned instrument - plucking my strings and getting the exact sound he wanted.

"What he always wants with a girl. He's offered too much money to waste time with the auction. He wants her, he gets her." He chews on the end of his cigar. "After your meeting this evening, I would think you'd understand she needs to be dealt with."

I'm staring at the screen. He's freeze-framed it for me.

Glancing at him, I recognize the smug grin for what it is. He thinks he's won.

I remember the same look as he stood over my mother's lifeless body. His hands covered in blood, the knife gripped in his right hand. I wasn't able to stop him then. I couldn't do anything at such a young age. But I'm not a child anymore.

"She'll be ready." Let him think he's still in control. My lesson was learned, that's what he wants. He thinks I've gotten to close to Magdalena, that I won't do my job because I don't treat her like he would.

Fuck. He's right on that point. I won't treat her like a useless whore. And there's no fucking way my girl is going to spend one second in the presence of that asshole Maksim.

"Good. If you are unable to complete the job, I'm sure we can help again." He walks away from me. He's had the last word, gave the last jab, and now he's dismissing me.

I don't say another word or look at the screen again. It's already burned into my mind. Never to leave.

I failed her.

I promised her no more forcing. I promised if she did what she was told, she wouldn't be punished.

"Get Dr. Morrow to my apartment now," I bark the order at the first servant girl I find. She nods, the fear showing in her eyes before she scatters off. I don't have time to play nice.

I bolt up the stairs and head to my apartment, making a mental checklist of everything that needs to happen next.

14

There's a soft humming around me. Voices, too. I ignore them both. The pain in my back has become more manageable, and I roll onto it, clinging to the blankets.

"The fuckers didn't even have a girl clean her up," I hear a growling voice say, but I just turn away from it. I don't want any more touching.

"We have to take the blanket off, dear." A soft voice penetrates through the fog, but I'm not fooled. I won't trust it, but I obey. There's no point in not. They'll just take it, and I'll be hurt again.

I don't want to be hurt anymore.

I kick off the blanket and spread my legs, sure they've come back for more. This is my life. A never-ending string of men who will fuck me at will and hurt me if I try to stop them.

"No, Magdalena." Rough hands push my knees together.

"I need to examine her," the soft voice says.

"After I clean her up."

A long sigh. "She's torn. I can see that already. She needs stitches this time. And the welts on her back are still bleeding. The stitches on her shoulder held, that's good at least."

Two arms slide beneath me. I hiss when my back is touched.

"I'll clean her quickly and bring her right back. Call for someone to get the bed changed. She's bled all over the sheets."

"I'll do it, hurry with cleaning her." The soft voice gets harder, but the touch to my knee is gentle.

I'm lifted in the air, but I don't glance at the man holding me. I don't care.

"Magdalena, look at me," the hard voice demands, and I turn to him, but focus on the stubble on his chin. He should shave. "Where do you hurt?"

I huff a laugh. It'd be easier to ask where I don't hurt.

He shifts me to my feet, and I hear water starting in the shower. I see the curtain, see him moving it out of the way and feel his hands on me, helping me into the stream, but it's so far above me I can't grasp it.

"Soap," he says and begins running hands over my body. I gasp when he brushes over my nipples. They're too sensitive. "Sorry," he mutters and keeps washing me. "Can you do your face?" he asks.

"Yeah," I say and hold out my hands. He looks familiar with his square jaw and dark eyes. I rub the soap into my hands until there's a thick lather then run them over my face. I can feel the crust on my cheeks and scratch it off with my fingernails. When I realize it's dry cum, I scratch harder.

"Hey, no. No, it's okay, Magdalena. You got it all." He pulls my hands away from my face. "Step in the water."

I listen. Because doing anything else will make him hurt me.

Once I'm clean, he dries me and plucks me back up in his arms.

"I can walk," I say but don't squirm to get free. I can, but I don't want to. It hurts between my legs and moving makes it worse.

"Put her down here," the soft voice says, and I look to where it's coming from. An older man, less stern looking, smiles gently at me.

The strong arms put me down on the bed.

"I need you to drop your knees to the side again, like you did before," the soft voice says, and I do what he says. He's poking and prodding me. New tears I didn't think were possible, roll down my cheeks.

"It's okay, Magdalena. Dr. Morrow won't hurt you. No one will hurt you ever again. I promise it," the stern voice says to me in Russian.

I cringe.

"Yes, they will," I say and turn away, letting the doctor do what he wants.

"She needs stitches, not many though," the doctor says. "I'll give you an antibiotic cream for the welts on her back and her butt."

"Her throat," the dark voice says and helps me to sit up slightly.

"Ah, yes." The doctor instructs me to open my mouth and a wooden stick is used to press my tongue out of his way. I gag and wince at the burning, raw pain. "There's a numbing spray that can be used, but I don't have any with me. I'll have to send out for it. Some pain relievers will help in the meantime. Soft foods until the swelling goes down. I don't see any lacerations, so that's good."

There's nothing good about this. About any of this.

"Send someone out to get it right away," the dark voice says again.

"Magdalena, do you remember who this

is?" the soft voice asks me. Apparently, he's a mind reader as well.

I remember, but I don't want to see him yet. I don't want to see anything yet.

"Magdalena, answer him."

I flinch at the harsh tone, but it gets me moving. "Yes. He's Kristoff."

"Very good."

"No, he's not good," I whisper and lean back against the pillows.

Silence stretches out across the room and I wonder if I've made him mad.

"I'm going to give you an injection now. It's going to numb you, so the stitches won't hurt." I look down the length of my body to where the doctor is holding a syringe.

"Will it make the pain inside go away too?" I ask.

The doctor shares a quick glance with Kristoff before answering me. "No, but I'll give you some other medicine to take care of that."

"Okay." I nod and lay back, staring up at the ceiling.

"I heard your father mention Maksim," the doctor says just before the pinprick of the needle digs into my sensitive, swollen flesh.

"It's not going to happen," Kristoff says with as much confidence as I've ever heard him use.

"He's not kind to his girls," the doctor presses on. I don't feel anything other than his presence. I can tell I'm being touched, but it doesn't hurt.

"I said it's not going to happen."

"You've taken to this one," the doctor says. I can feel the tension building in Kristoff and I close my eyes, not wanting to see his anger.

"She's mine," is all Kristoff says. But if I was really his, would those other men have taken me? Touched me and forced me the way they did?

When I peek at him, I see a sadness. He looks down at me, his dark eyes full of remorse and worry. There's a deep crease in his forehead.

If he dislikes me so much, if he would hurt me so easily why is he looking at me with so much guilt and concern? The last time he'd been with me, before the men took me, he'd been almost sweet. He'd offered to find me something to do to pass the time while he was away doing work. He hadn't forced me since that first time, he'd been demanding, hard, and unrelenting in his authority, but he hadn't hurt me again. Not like those men.

It's then I realize Kristoff had been kept from me. He wouldn't have allowed it to happen if he'd been here, if he'd known. He would have kept them from hurting me. He would have protected me if he had been aware. It's why his father didn't include him, didn't have him in the room. Kristoff would have protected me.

I reach my hand out and wrap my fingers around his, letting the warmth of his touch fill me. Closing my eyes again, I hold onto him while the doctor finishes his work.

He squeezes my hand when the doctor finishes and my legs are closed again. The movements hurt but are dulled by his touch.

"Here's the cream for her back. I'll let you do it. Make sure you watch those welts, so she doesn't get an infection. I'll check on the stitches in a few days and should be able to remove them. She can't be used until then, Kristoff." The last sentence is firm.

"No one will touch her," Kristoff declares and lets go of my hand to pull fresh covers over my body.

"It will take her a little time," I hear the doctor say, but I'm not sure what he means. I close my eyes again, trying to find that little corner where I can hide. I don't want to think about the pain, or how it came to life, or where I am, or where I'm going.

"She's stronger than she thinks," Kristoff states and a door is closed. A bolt slides in place.

Kristoff walks over to the side of the bed

again and sits down. "I have to rub this on your back. It's going to sting," he says, showing me the tube of ointment the doctor gave him. He sounds sorry already and he hasn't touched me yet.

"Okay," I nod, but he keeps staring at me.

His lips crack into a gentle smile. "You have to roll onto your stomach, Magdalena," he says.

Right. I knew that.

I manage the feat without causing more pain to my aching muscles and sink into the pillow once I'm face down.

The blanket is pulled down and I fist the pillows. I jump at the first touch of his finger to my skin.

"No!" I yell and scramble up to my knees.

"Magdalena, it's just me and it's okay. See, just the ointment." He holds up the tube again. "Just the medicine to help you heal."

I shake my head, clearing away the fuzz.

"Right. Yeah. Okay," I say and slink back into position.

I clench my eyes while he liberally applies the ointment to the welts. There has to be many of them because he curses when he sees my back.

"I will kill them all." His vow is spoken low and in Russian. This wouldn't have happened if he had been here. He would have stopped them. I can feel it, know it deep down. He wouldn't have let them hurt me.

"Where were you?" I ask, swallowing over the soreness of my throat.

"On a fool's errand," he says with heat. "I have questions for you, but it will wait until tomorrow." The definitive tone doesn't suggest I push for more answers, and I'm too tired to argue. Too sore to tempt his anger. Though a sense of safety spreads through me with his touch. He's being gentle and when I hiss from his touch on a sensitive spot he apologizes.

"Will the man I'm sold to do this? Will he do what Andrei did?" I ask softly, feeling the tears wet my lashes. I don't want to know, but I have to ask. I can't go around blindly anymore. The hope I held onto is gone, and I can't be foolish enough to try to regain it.

Kristoff doesn't answer. The cap snaps closed on the tube of medicine and he pulls the sheet over my naked ass. The ointment sticks to the sheet, but I don't tell him. He's giving me privacy, at least a small pinch of it, and I'm going to take it. Because I know in a few days I won't have any.

"I've heard of Maksim. My sister's mentioned him." He's a monster is what I want to say, but I don't. I had called Kristoff a monster, but I had been wrong. His father, the men who hurt me, they are beasts from hell. Maksim is more like them.

"Don't worry about that Russian fuck. He won't get near you." He gives me another vow. But I know he can't keep these promises.

"Another buyer?" I ask. I'm talking about my one sale like I'm inquiring into the sale of a car.

"No." The word is said with force, a finality.

But I guess I still haven't learned, because I press on. "So, then Maksim will buy me, and he'll do what these men did." I close my eyes. "And more," I whisper.

He wipes the hair from my face and brings his nose to touch mine. "No. No Magdalena. No one will hurt you. Never again. I promise. These men that did this - I will kill them all. Maksim will never see you, never touch you."

His breath is hot against my skin. I take a deep breath, willing my heart to believe him. To find the speck of hope I'd been holding onto. But it's gone. He can't promise these things, even if he means them.

"In two days, I'll be sold," I say softly, leaning into him, wanting his touch to wash away the bad memories, to take away the feeling of grime those men put on me.

"No. You're mine, Magdalena," he says harshly. "You aren't going anywhere, with anyone."

His lips press to mine, stealing away my next sentence. The contradiction to his promise, the truth. I will be sold and taken away from him. But his kiss is more powerful. He's twisting my thoughts, turning them away from the fear and pushing them to him.

"You aren't going anywhere. I swear it to you," he whispers in English. "I will kill anyone who touches you." Another vow, another promise for him to break, but I can't take away the hope from him. I don't want him to feel this despair, this emptiness. So, I say nothing.

Because for this moment, I have him. And I don't hate him. I lean into him and he climbs into the bed, cradling my head to his chest.

"Sleep now, Magdalena," he orders in that overbearing way of his, but even if I wanted to disobey him, my eyes are already closing.

15

I bring up a tray of scrambled eggs and yogurt for Magdalena the morning after my father's men sealed their fates. No servants are allowed in my apartment now, no one here is to be trusted.

Dr. Morrow found the spray to help numb her throat, but she won't let me give it to her. She swears it's not so bad this morning, but I think she's relying on the pain for a safe place to hide.

She didn't fight me when I reapplied the ointment, or when I helped her to the bathroom. I was both pleased and worried. It seems the fight has left her completely. No matter how much I try to pull her back from it, she's comfortable sitting in the darkness.

I showed it to her when I took her ass, and now she finds it comforting.

When I enter my bedroom, she's standing by the windows, her arms crossed over her chest. Every angry welt is on display. They are already turning to ugly purple and blue streaks crisscrossing her shoulder blades and her ass. I see at least two across the bottom of her back and grind my teeth together. They could have damaged her kidneys with their carelessness.

"I've brought breakfast," I say when she doesn't move to look at me. Her hair is damp.

"I'm not really hungry. Is it okay if I wait to eat?" she asks softly. Where is the feisty woman who would simply tell me to fuck off with the tray?

"No, you need to eat something." I'm taking advantage of her warped sense of submission, but I don't care. She's lost weight since she's been with me, and she's been battered and bruised.

She sighs but comes to me anyway. I can see the movements still pain her, but she doesn't comment on it. I help her sit in the chair at the table and hand her the spoon. "At least the yogurt. It's softer and shouldn't hurt your throat too much."

"Okay." She sinks the spoon into the vanilla yogurt.

I take the chair across from her and study her eating. She's taking small bites and each time she swallows, I can tell it hurts. She'll have ice cream for lunch, I decide. And I'm going to rip out the fucking throats of those men.

"I need to ask you a few questions. You need to be honest with me," I say with a hardness forced into my tone. She responds better to it, and I need her cooperation if I'm going to sort out everything and get my plan into action.

She nods and takes another bite.

"When is the last time you spoke to your sister?" I ask, folding my hands in my lap and crossing my ankle over my knee.

"I talk with her every day. So, the day before I was taken." Her voice is still hoarse but at least she doesn't wince every time she speaks.

"I mean talk. When's the last time you talked?" I ask again.

Her brow furrows. "What do you mean? I just told you."

"I looked through your phone. You've texted her almost daily, but I didn't see her in your call list. So, when's the last time you actually talked to her, heard her voice, saw her?" I have information for her, and it's going to hurt. She's going to be knocked for a loop, so I need to bring her to the conclusion herself, or at least as close to it as possible. Maybe it will soften the reality.

Though nothing has been soft about her reality since she's come into my world.

"She's busy," she says defensively. "She's not even in the country most of the time," she goes on to explain.

"When?" I ask again. My patience is slipping.

She heaves a heavy sigh and takes another bite of her yogurt. "Why does it matter? She won't find me in time." Does she think that I'm trying to track down Danuta because I'm afraid she'll show up and ruin everything?

"It matters because I've asked." I manage to keep my voice even.

When she looks at me, it's with a serene acceptance. The hope that burned so annoyingly in her days ago has fizzled out.

"A month, maybe more. But she texts back most of the time."

Most of the time? After skimming through her phone, I've become more obsessed with her relationship with her sister. Every day Magdalena texts her sister with an update on what she's up to and asks Danuta about her day. Maybe - and I'm being extremely generous - Danuta answers her a quarter of the time.

"Your sister's older than you and your parents died when you were young, is that right?" I ask.

"Why are you asking all this if you already know?" She sounds irritated. Good. "My parents were killed in an accident when I was in high school. Since Danuta was legal age, she was given guardianship, so I wouldn't go to a group home. Once I went to college, she transferred out of the local police department and went into the CIA."

All of this, I already knew.

"Did Danuta know you were coming to England to track down my father?"

She nods. "Yeah. I told her where I'd be, gave her the address of the apartment I found."

"So, she knew you were coming to expose my father's business?"

"Yeah. She didn't like it, told me it was too dangerous. I explained I was only getting a story from the outside. I wouldn't have any contact with him or any of his people." She stops talking and laughs. "Which apparently was incorrect."

I reach over the table and pat her hand. "Focus on me, Magdalena. Forget yesterday."

Forget? She'll never forget, but I'll do my damnedest to give her something better to focus on.

She slips her hand out from beneath mine and picks up the glass of water I brought her. She wanted orange juice, but her throat is too raw, it would have been painful.

"When your father dies, and you take over the business, do you think you'll keep the same business model?" she asks in prime journalist voice.

The question catches me off guard, but I quickly recover.

"I'm not going to take over my father's business." It's not a lie. I'm not. I have other ventures that will make me just as much money.

"Hmm." She sips her water.

She doesn't believe me. Fine. She's getting me off topic anyway, and I need to get this going or everything I have planned will be delayed.

"Have you thought about how my father's men knew where you were? And who you were?"

"They thought I was my sister," she shrugs.

"How'd they know where you were?"

"I don't know," she sounds annoyed with my questions. I can see the fatigue in her eyes, but I have to get this done before she can nap.

"Danuta isn't coming to save you, Magdalena."

A dark cloud crosses her expression. "I already know that." She drops the spoon onto the tray.

My phone dings seven times in secession. I check the messages. Things are falling into place. Good.

"I'm going to move you from my room. I have a man coming who's going to take you to a safe place. You have to stay with him until I come for you, okay? You can't try to escape, and you can't go with anyone else. Do you understand that?"

She shakes her head. Of course, she doesn't understand.

I leave the table and bring her a pile of clothes. Some leggings and a sweater I snagged from Tricia.

"Clothes?" she asks like I'm offering her a million-dollar security bond.

"Yes. You're back and ass will still be a bit tender, but I can't have you walking around naked now." I try to smile, but the fear in her eyes kills my attempt at levity.

"You're sending me away. Does that mean the sale will happen now?" Her voice is shaking. How many times have I heard the same tremor and ignored it?

I deserve the hell I'm destined for.

"Magdalena, I told you. You aren't being sold. You're staying with me, but for right now I need you to go with Carlos. He's going to keep you safe for me until I come get you."

She blinks. "No."

"No?" I can't help the sharpness of my tone. She's back to defying me again. While a good sign, still irritating.

"No. I'm not going anywhere. I'm not going with Carlos or your father or anyone else. I'm staying right fucking here." She slams her hand on the table and stands up.

"Magdalena, I need you to listen to me now. No fucking around. You have to do exactly as I say." My phone chimes again. He's early, but I can't argue with the time. I trust Carlos. He's the only one I can now. My father's men - my men - could turn on me for this. I can't chance her safety.

"Who is he?" she asks, folding her arms over her chest.

"What?" I want to shake her; doesn't she understand how much time we don't have?

"Who is he?" she parrots herself.

"A man I've known for a very long time. He's loyal only to me." Well, and his own family who would gladly slit my father's throat if given the chance. But we don't have time for all the particulars.

"I don't want him touching me." The demand is still there, lingering with the twinge of fear, but I know her little tells. And she's avoiding my eyes, she's staring at my chin again. She's terrified.

"He won't," I promise. He might have to if she freaks out and tries to run, but I'm keeping that information to myself.

She stares at me, at the pile of clothes in my hands and after a long moment she nods and takes them from me. I try to help her, but she swats my hands away.

"When this is all over and you're back to yourself, we're going to talk about appropriate behavior," I mutter to myself, but make sure she overhears me. Her eyes snap to me, and for a moment I'm afraid I've made her retreat back inside herself. The soft blush blossoming on her cheeks tell me there's hope. She's still in there.

While she's working her way into the clothes, I leave her to open my apartment door. Carlos is waiting outside looking as much of a bastard as ever. He has more tattoos than skin I think, and his shaved head shimmers from the overhead lighting.

"Fuck, you're going to terrify her," I say, slapping his back when he walks into my room.

"No more than you, my friend," he says with a nod. "I have the place ready. Are those jackasses downstairs going to give me trouble?" he asks, jerking a finger at the front door.

"No. I'll take you two down the back exit. If we run into anyone, I'll handle it." I look toward the bedroom door. I hadn't locked it and now it's opening. Magdalena is standing in the doorway, her hair pulled back into a slick ponytail and her feet bare. Shit.

"Shoes." I hold up a finger and run to the closet.

"You're Carlos?" she asks in her journalist voice again.

"I am." Carlos doesn't move toward her.

"Why would you help Kristoff get me away from his father? From Maksim. You know either of them would kill you for doing it." She's not wrong.

Carlos isn't the sort to let a little threat of death stop him. "I owe Kristoff my sister's life, and my own. If I die helping him, so be it."

I grab her shoes from my closet. Her clothes had been cut from her when she was brought in, but I saved the shoes.

"Why do you owe him?" she asks when I hand her the shoes.

"He'll tell you later, get these on." I point to the shoes. I move around the room, grabbing everything I need. A second gun, more ammo, and a burner phone.

"I think I should know now," she says, still not moving.

My teeth snap, and I take a deep breath. "Magdalena, I'm trying here, baby. I'm trying to keep my cool, but if you don't start listening to me in three seconds, I'm going to have to find a way to punish you. And I can't spank you, so my options are going to be a bit more sinister."

A shudder runs through her body. I saw it. Her pupils dilate, and her chest thrusts out. Ah. There's my girl.

"Whatever." She snorts and moves to the couch to stuff her feet into the shoes.

I grin at Carlos. "Call me as soon as you get to the location." I throw him the burner. "I won't make a move until I know she's safe."

"You sure you got this?" he asks me. "Going up against your father - you can't come back from that shit."

"I don't want to. And I'm not going against him, I'm taking him down," I explain.

"My men are waiting for your signal. Once you give it, they'll charge in."

I nod and grab his hand to shake appreciatively. He's taking a big risk here. His men may not make it home after this.

I swirl the silencer into place on my gun and grab Magdalena's hand, pulling her along through my apartment to the back hall. She's never seen outside my bedroom, aside from the dungeon. And she never will. Once this is done, we are never coming back here.

We make our way down the back stairwell without any trouble. Carlos' car is just outside the gates, and we manage to get there without meeting anyone. My father is confident that everything is going as planned. His stunt yesterday with Magdalena has him thinking he's put me back in my place.

"Kristoff? What are you doing?" Viktor calls out to us. When my eyes land on him, the blood drains from his face. He knows I know. Frantically, he looks from me to Magdalena then back. "Look, man, she - fuck, your father said - I had no fucking choice," he cries like a beggar.

I step away from Carlos and Magdalena, making my way over to him. He's in a panic, and he fucking should be. He should be running away, but he's a fucking idiot and stands still, waiting for me to come to him. Did he think I'd forgive him?

When I'm close enough, I throw the heel of my hand into his nose. The crunch isn't satisfying enough, nor is the scream of pain he unleashes. Once he's on the ground, holding his nose, I point my gun and shoot through his neck. His cries are garbled. Blood pours from his wound, but it's not a fatal shot. Just enough to shut him up.

I step over him, straddling his chest and squat down to look into his face. "You thought you could touch what's mine and live?" I ask, but don't expect an answer.

KRISTOFF: BLAIRE'S WORLD

He's grabbing for his throat, wiggling beneath me in pain.

Moving down the length of his body, I press the silencer to his groin. I look up at him, catch his horrified look as I pull the trigger, sending a bullet through his balls. I send another one through. Blood pours from his groin onto the gravel beneath him.

Between the neck wound, and groin, he's going to live another few minutes. Long enough to feel every bit of the pain I put him in. But just to be sure, I press the heel of my boot to the wound. Stepping on his balls makes his body shudder with pain. He's lost too much blood now to do much else but lie there and moan.

"Kristoff! C'mon," Carlos calls me.

I shove my boot into Viktor's groin one last time, not getting any reaction out of his lifeless eyes, and turn back to Carlos and Magdalena.

Her eyes are on me and her mouth is parted.

"I told you I'll kill them all. They will all pay," I say to her and press a kiss to her cheek. "Now, let's go."

We get to Carlos's car and I get her strapped in with no arguments from her. She's still staring at me like she's just seeing me for the first time.

"Magdalena, you listen to Carlos okay?

Don't fight him, even if what he asks you to do seems scary, okay? He's going to keep you safe until I come for you."

She nods. "You'll come for me."

"Right." I press another kiss to her forehead. "I love you. I need you to know that before you go." Because there's a chance she may not see me again, I may not survive this attack.

Her brow furrows again in confusion.

"I know, it makes no fucking sense to me either, but it's true." I look at Carlos and nod. "You listen to him, or you'll answer to me when I see you."

She starts to say something, but I close the door. If it's an argument, I won't listen to it anyway, and if she's going to tell me how she feels about me, I don't want to know. A monster like me doesn't deserve such an innocent angel like her.

16

We make it through the main gates of the property, but I can sense Carlos getting nervous. He's checking the rearview mirror too often.

"What's wrong?" I ask, my stomach rolling with nausea.

"Nothing, everything's fine," he says and looks over his shoulder at the cars behind us in traffic.

"Doesn't seem that way," I say wondering why Kristoff would put me in this man's care if he was so skittish.

"Everything's—"

A high pitch squeal hits my ears just before the crunch of metal. I'm thrown to the right, straight into Carlos. The car is dragged up the sidewalk and into a pole.

I hear Carlos screaming, but I can't see

him. Where is he? A woman walks up to us, while I struggle to get out of my belt. My door has caved in. Blood covers my shirt on my side, and the pain is unreal, but I have to get out.

"Carlos!" I call for him. He's on the sidewalk outside the car, glass is sticking out of his arm.

A woman walks up to the car. Her hair is pulled back, silver-blond, and tied off behind her neck. She's wearing thick round sunglasses, so I can't see her eyes when she sticks her head through my window. Shards of glass cover me. Her car is still wedged into my door.

"Help my friend," I say pointing to him. She looks past me to where Carlos is starting to get to his feet.

"Sure," she says and leaves me, walks around the car to where he's scrambling to his feet.

She looks familiar, her walk, her voice. I shout a warning, but it's too late. Carlos is shot in the head. Blood sprays the sidewalk, his legs spasm then go quiet, but I'm still screaming. And stuck. I can't get the fucking seat belt off of me.

The woman yanks his door open more and bends to look at me. "C'mon sis, we got to go." She flashes me a smile. One I've seen millions of times since I was born.

"Danuta?" I ask, unbelieving.

"Let's go, Maggie, I'm on a schedule here." She points her gun at me. My sister. I'm her fucking sister, and she's pointing a gun at me.

"Danuta, what are you doing?" I ask, making my way over the center console of the car. The gear shift shoves into my hip and I curse. There isn't an inch of me that doesn't hurt.

She grabs hold of my arm and pulls me out. I stumble but manage to get to my feet. I check my side, pulling the tear in the sweater open to see the wound from the door. A nasty gash is bleeding. I hiss and press hard against it.

"Let's go," she says again and pulls me away from the wreck. I glance over my shoulder, at Carlos. He said he owed Kristoff a great debt, but I doubt his life was worth it.

I don't fight Danuta. She's my big sister. She'll have a reason for what she's done.

She puts me in the front seat of her car, a large black SUV that has taken minimal damage from ramming the Volvo Carlos drove. Once the door is slammed shut, I lean back against the seat.

"He was helping me," I tell her when she's pulled the SUV away from the accident, leaving Carlos alone and bleeding all over the pavement.

"No, he wasn't. That's why I killed him," she says so casually the words don't compute at first.

"No, he was. How do you know?" I ask, shaking my head. "Danuta, why would you—"

She sighs in frustration. "You really are a fucking idiot, Maggie. I told you to stay away from here. Didn't I?" she smacks her hand against the steering wheel and gives me a glare.

"You did." I nod. "My side hurts. It's cut bad," I say, looking down at the blood staining the sweater.

She barely glances before turning down another road, picking up speed. "Carlos wasn't helping you, he was taking you to another safe house where he'd keep you until it was time for you to be transported to Maksim."

"What? No. Kristoff said he trusted him." I rub my head. I'm getting so dizzy and she's talking too fast.

"Of course, he did. That's why Andrei paid Carlos a shit ton of money to take you and hide you from Kristoff until the sale was complete." She turns down another road and I hit the door from the severity of the turn.

She can't be telling the truth. Kristoff wouldn't give me to someone that would double cross him.

"How do you know this?" I ask, holding onto the dashboard when she takes the next turn, so I don't hit my side again.

"Because." It's the only answer I get.

"You said you weren't looking into Andrei right now, you told me you were focusing on a larger ring in Russia." I remember the last real conversation we had - months ago.

"Just relax. We're almost there," she says and flips her phone out of her back pocket and starts a call.

"I have her. No, she thinks I'm saving her. It's fine. Yes, I'm about to enter the tunnel, I'll be there in five minutes," she speaks in Russian.

She doesn't know I learned the language. I never told her. After I finished college, she was so busy with work we rarely had real conversations. I must not have told her - or she's forgotten.

"Who was that?" I ask, letting her stick with her misconception.

"My partner. He's going to meet us just through here." She points at the tunnel coming up.

Too many scenarios run through my head. Who's telling me the truth? Did Carlos work for Andrei or was he truly loyal to Kristoff? Why would Danuta pretend to help me? Isn't she the good guy? She's CIA for fuck's sake.

The darkness of the tunnel clears and we're pulling into an underground lot. Danuta parks the car and hops out of her side. I push open my door and gingerly start to move, but then she's there, yanking me to my feet.

I cry out from the pain, but she doesn't notice. Or she doesn't care. She takes me into a building, and we bypass two men standing guard at the main door. I get a quick glance, but I recognize them. They are Andrei's men.

I yank back on her hold, but she's ready for it and pulls out her gun.

"It would be a shame to have to lug your dead body all the way down the hall," she says with her teeth clenched together.

I'm pulled into a room, the same room I woke up in when Andrei had kidnapped me. The smell hasn't changed. But the captive in the chair has.

"Andrei!" Danuta lets me go and runs to him. His eyes are both swollen shut, he can't see her. His hands are bound behind him and his jaw is bruised.

Someone has beaten him and left him for her to find him.

"Who did this? Where are your men? Why haven't they come in to help you?"

KRISTOFF: BLAIRE'S WORLD

Danuta rattles off her questions like a hysterical girlfriend.

Andrei mouths words, they come out jumbled and more like dolphin sounds. Getting frustrated with himself, he sticks out his tongue. The front half has been cut off.

My stomach rolls and I take a step back, holding my belly and taking deep breaths.

Danuta only gasps at the sight before she starts to work the ties on his hands. "Who? Your bastard son?" she demands, and he nods.

"I assure you my father was married to my mother when she gave birth to me." Kristoff walks in the open door. Blood covers his shirt and his arms. I press myself against the wall, unsure of where to go. "He was also married to her when he cut out her tongue and beat her to death."

I sink to the floor, grappling for something to keep me upright. The dizziness is getting worse.

"Kristoff. You can't do this. He's your father. You have a duty," Danuta rants at him, waving her gun at him.

Kristoff walks to her as though the gun won't end his life if she raises it just a hair higher and pulls the trigger.

"You speak of duty? Your duty was to your sister. To raise her and care for her and protect her. And what did you do? You sold her! You gave her over to Andrei, so he could make money off of her, and you could be rid of her."

I watch my sister, waiting for her to deny his accusations. He can't be telling the truth.

"You don't know anything."

"Your parents left you both a trust fund. And once Magdalena turns twenty-five, she'll inherit a million dollars. Just like you did. But if she dies - the money's yours."

"No. Kristoff, there's no money." I shake my head and push myself back to my feet.

He stiffens at my voice but doesn't turn to me.

"There's no money, right Danuta? You would have told me," I say, knowing after seeing her eyes frantically look for a place to run, that Kristoff is telling me the truth.

"I don't understand." I stumble and grab my side. The bleeding has slowed, but the pain is there - so much pain. Kristoff looks at me then, seeing the damage done to me and his face hardens.

Before I can explain, before I can plead, he pulls his hand back and whips his knife at my sister, striking her square in her chest. She staggers back, a look of shocked horror frozen on her face as she falls to the ground.

I scream and try to run to her, but Kristoff holds me back. She's dead. She probably was before she hit the ground, his aim was spot on - straight to her heart.

Air won't come to me, I can't get it inside my body. Crumbling to the ground, Kristoff sets me against the wall. "Don't look, baby. Don't look," he says and leaves me, pulling another knife from his pants.

I can't see past him. Kristoff blocks my view of Andrei, but it only takes a second for me to know what's happening. A strangled cry and then it's over, blood pours down to the floor, pooling around the chair, over Kristoff's boots. Like a river, it heads for my sister and mingles with her blood now flooding around her body.

She's dead. My sister didn't save me.

Kristoff wipes his knife off on his father's suit jacket and re-sheaths it. He steps to me, squats down.

"It's over now, baby. All over." He sounds soothing. Like I should be happy. I should be calm.

I look at my sister, lying lifeless and limp. So much blood.

My stomach rolls and I fall to my side just as the contents are emptied on the floor. A fire burns in my side and I whimper, but I have no more energy for screaming.

Sleep. I want sleep. Long hours, days, months even. As long as it takes for time to rewind and for all of this to go back to normal.

KRISTOFF: BLAIRE'S WORLD

Back to when my sister was just a CIA agent too busy to talk to her little sister. Back to when I was scrounging around places I shouldn't have been to try and get a story. Before I bought plane tickets to England. Before I heard of Andrei Dowidoff.

"It's okay, I have you," Kristoff says, but I'm too far away to respond. Playing in the darkness.

Dark is good.

It hides me so well.

I think I'll stay here for a while.

17

Dr. Morrow waits for me in my office. He's helping himself to a glass of vodka from my wet bar when I enter.

He finishes pouring when he notices me and offers me one.

I shake my head. No amount of vodka will take the edge off.

"Is she safe?" I ask, throwing myself into my chair. My father's old chair. I hate it, it's lumpy and caved in from where his ass made a groove. I'll replace it later. Once I'm finished tying up the loose ends.

Dr. Morrow nods. "She's been admitted to Mount Sinai. I have access to her records and the attending physician is keeping me updated. She'll be just fine once she wakes up."

I don't like medical induced coma's, no

matter how much Dr. Morrow tries to convince me they are safe. It scares the hell out of me, but she never would have gotten on that plane willingly.

"The gash on her side?" I ask, trying to block out the image of all the blood saturating her sweater. She lost so much of it, Dr. Morrow was surprised she'd been conscious for as long as she had been.

"Deeper than I would have liked to see her travel with, but the stitches held. She lost a lot of blood, though, Kristoff. She'll need some time to recover."

"And her other injuries?" I'm listing these items like I'm getting a report on projects I've asked him to handle. I'll deal with the reality of it all later. Once he's gone and I can finish what needs to be done. Then I can drown myself in vodka.

"All healing. They'll wake her tomorrow. I'll know more then." He assures me everything's going to be fine for her, but he can only answer the physical questions. Magdalena was put through hell while here. The mind can only handle so much horror, so much betrayal.

"Once she's released, I want her set up with the best therapist in New York. She's to have round the clock access for help."

Dr. Morrow's brows shoot up. "She's going to be very confused, Kristoff, and while I agree she'll need someone to help her sort out everything that happened to her while she was here - she's going to need answers. And she's not going to like waking up to find you've left her." His voice is that of a chastising old woman trying to guilt me into doing the right thing.

But I did the right thing. I protected her, I saved her from those that would see her dead, then I sent her away.

"Seeing me would only be a reminder. She needs to figure out a way to forget." I push off the chair. I think about her too much, and this conversation is only needling a wound I can't treat. There is no fixing it, and I don't deserve for it to be cleaned and bandaged. I deserve the pain and the infection. Because that's what I am. An infection. If I were to stay with her. If I hadn't sent her back to New York, I would have festered in her life and destroyed her. I've already stolen her innocence, I won't be responsible for ruining everything else.

"I don't think she'll agree," he says into his glass as he takes a sip.

"You're probably right, but it's not up to her. I know what's best for her and I'm taking care of it." I sound like a man who has any right to make decisions on her behalf. I don't. I've not earned that privilege. But fuck it, I don't care. I won't allow any more hurt to come to her. And all I bring is pain.

"She'll need assistance dealing with her sister's estate," he reminds me of another item on my list. Danuta. CIA agent turned human trafficker. It still boggles me. My father complained about the Americans getting their nose into everything for years. Danuta was a particular thorn in his side. Apparently, it only took the scent of money to lure that bitch away from the rest of her pack.

"Put a man on it. I don't want her to have to deal with anything on her own. She's to have full support. Get her an apartment, she gave up the one she had when she came here for her story." After everything that's happened, I'm still irritated that she'd been so foolish in coming to England to snoop around. "I want the rent paid for the year, and after that, if she wants to stay, I want the bill paid. She's not to want for anything, do you understand?"

He nods in agreement. I've given him duties well outside his physician skills, but he'll see it's done.

"She'll have questions," he prods me again.

I head to the door. Talking about her has made the dark cloud appear again, and I need to finish what I started downstairs.

"She'll have a roof over her head, and safety. That's all she needs." I yank the door open and head to the stairwell.

As I head down to the pits of the house, I can already hear the moans and cries of the four men I have waiting for me. Peeling off my shirt, I head into the first room. Into the cell I'd kept Magdalena when she first arrived. Matvei is restrained, facing away from me in the cell, his naked ass greeting me when I walk in.

"Are you ready?" I ask him.

"Kristoff," he pleads, frantically trying to turn his face to me, but he's already received some of his punishment. He can't see me, no matter where he looks. One eye has swollen shut, the other has been cut out.

"I asked if you're ready," I say again, firmer, and pull out the knife I've brought with me.

"I was only doing what your father told me to do! I followed orders!" he cries, tears are already falling. Fucking pussy.

His legs have been cuffed to the cell bars, spread wide open for me. I reach between them and pull his cock back toward me. I squeeze the soft shaft and pull downward.

"No! No!" he screams and tries to wiggle away. He's fighting hard, and if he weren't restrained so well, he might actually get away. But I'm not a novice. And he's earned every bit of this.

The knife slices easily through him, and his dick falls to the ground. His screams are deafening now, but I'm not done. Blood pours out, and if I take too long, he might pass out from the blood loss before I finish. And I don't want that to happen.

Magdalena didn't get to sleep through the five men raping and beating her. They will not get the convenience either.

I pull one ass cheek to the side and line up the tip of my knife to his clenched ass hole. He's still hollering over losing his cock, I'm not sure if he even realizes what's coming next.

"Shhhh," I say soothingly. "Shhh, Matvei. Almost done." He stills for a moment, like he's trying to hear me, trying to figure out what's next. And he does, as my knife slowly begins to enter his ass.

"No!" He bucks again, but it's no use. I had planned to go slow, but he's getting annoying, so I shove the knife up into him.

"Does that feel good, Matvei?" I ask, reminding myself of how scared Magdalena must have been. How much pain he and his friends brought her. I twist the knife and pull downward, toward his dismembered cock. The knife tears him apart, his balls are ripped open and blood splatters over my boots.

I wait for him to stop shouting and collapse into his binds. He probably still has a pulse, but not for long. I remove my knife, wiping it on his shirt until it's clean and step back.

Lifeless, he dangles from his binds.

I step out of the room, signaling one of my men to clean up the mess. I have three more rooms to play in. I sheath my knife and roll my shoulders. It's going to be a long morning.

18

Six Months Later…

The beat of the music mirrors my heart pounding in my chest. It's not my first time at The Dungeon, my favorite play space in New York. I've been here every week over the past two months. There's no reason for my nerves to be so on edge.

It's been six months since I woke up in that damn hospital bed. Alone and scared.

Physically, I'm all healed. It's the rest of me that's fucked up.

Kristoff abandoned me - threw me away.

His men tried to explain things the way he'd told them to, I'm sure. He's paid for an apartment, that I won't stay in. He's hired the best therapist in New York for me, who I won't speak to. And he's taken care of all my sister's estate issues leaving me with an overflowing bank account - which I won't touch.

I didn't lose a sister when his knife penetrated her heart, I'd lost her years ago. I don't know everything; the government doesn't like to admit it when one of their own goes off the grid and joins a human trafficking ring. I learned everything I needed to know when I got my hands on her laptop. She'd joined up with Andrei over a year ago. Just when the investigation turned to focus elsewhere. How convenient.

Kristoff had been right about the trust fund. On my twenty-fifth birthday, I will gain full access to it. But he was wrong about the amount. Interest compounds and it's been sitting there for ten years. It's close to five million now, and I'll have it in another month.

When I questioned the attorney in charge of the funds, why I hadn't been notified when I turned eighteen, he didn't have an answer. Danuta knew who to pay off.

Officially, Danuta was killed while investigating Andrei Dowidoff - who had been killed by one of his own men. Matvei's picture had been plastered between Danuta and Andrei's in the NY Times. While my sister was being touted as a hero, I was piecing my life back together.

"Hey, Mags," Bobby, a Dominant I

played with casually before, says. Before Kristoff. Before everything.

"Hi." I force a smile. We've played several times over the past weeks, and I'm looking forward to tonight. He promised a hard session, and I'm going to hold him to it. I need the bite of pain and he's been holding back, afraid I wasn't ready. He doesn't know anything about what happened in England. But he thinks the death of my sister is taking me a while to work out.

His brown eyes dart toward the lobby. "Did you make plans tonight?"

"I don't have any plans," I insist. "If you want to play with someone else, that's fine—"

"No, it's not that." He looks over my outfit - a short cut black dress and bites his lip. "No, it's not that at all. But there's a guy at the entrance looking for you."

I turn to see what he's pointing at.

Dr. Morrow.

My stomach flips. Something's happened to Kristoff.

"Do you want me to get rid of him?" Bobby asks in that protective tone of his that used to get me wet just listening to. But, like everything else we've done over the past weeks, it's not enough.

"No. I know him. He's a friend. I'll just talk to him real quick and come back." I keep my eyes locked on Dr. Morrow and leave Bobby standing near the bar.

Dr. Morrow cracks a gentle smile when I approach him.

"Sorry, Magdalena, he's not vetted," John, the guard at the door, tells me.

"I know. It's fine. I'll step out." I walk past Dr. Morrow and motion for him to follow me to the lobby, and out to the street.

"What's wrong?" I ask immediately once we're outside. I wrap my arms around myself to ward off the chill.

"I don't think Kristoff would approve of your dress," he says and shakes off his coat, draping it over my shoulders.

"Approve?" I shake my head. "What's wrong, why are you here?" I ask, more demanding, but I'm trying to keep my heart from leaping out of my chest.

"Nothing is wrong. I promise," he says in that gentle voice of his. How anyone so calm and sweet could work for the Dowidoff family makes no sense to me.

"Then why did you just try to get into The Dungeon? And break up my date?"

"That man was your date?" he asks with raised brows. "He didn't seem very - well, your type."

If he means Bobby's nothing like Kristoff, he's right. They couldn't be more different. One believes in consent and limits, while the other just takes what he wants when he wants.

"Kristoff wasn't my choice, Dr. Morrow," I remind him.

His lips press firmly into a straight line. "Yes, I know, but you came to care for him anyway." I didn't need that reminder. Not tonight.

"If every thing's okay, why did you track me down?" I push for an answer. It's cold, and I don't want Bobby to find another partner.

"Kristoff is in town. He wants to see you," he says on a long breath.

"So, he sent a messenger?" I laugh. "I have nothing to say to him." Or everything. I have everything to say, to cry, to feel with him, but I can't do it. I can't allow myself to fall into him again. It was wrong, having feelings for him. He was my captor. It was sick and twisted, and now I'm home, I'm free, and I'm not going to fall for him again.

"No, not exactly," Dr. Morrow says as a black SUV pulls up to the curb beside us. My stomach twists and the little hairs on the back of my neck stand up.

The back door opens, and Kristoff is sitting there. His expression dark, like he's not as happy to see me as Dr. Morrow's tone suggested.

"Magdalena. Get in," he says and waves

me to his side.

I laugh again and slip Dr. Morrow's coat off me. "I'm not going anywhere with you." I hand the coat back to the doctor who looks worried now. When I turn back to Kristoff, I can see why. He's taken one look at my outfit and is climbing out of the car.

"I asked you to get in the car." Kristoff yanks the coat back from the doctor and throws it over my shoulders.

"No. You told me. And I'm not getting in the fucking car, Kristoff." I stand my ground but keep the coat. He'll be easier to deal with if I'm covered up.

"Who are you here with?" he demands and looks back at the entrance to the club.

"No one." It's not a complete lie. Bobby and I had planned to play, but we aren't a couple. He's probably found someone else to play with by now.

"Then why won't you get in?" he asks. I don't think anyone has ever told him no and gotten away with it, he seems confused by the concept.

"Because I'm not ready to leave yet, and I don't want to see you." I keep my eyes averted from his gaze. Being caught in that dominant glare of his will make my resolve weaken.

"Maybe, Magdalena would agree to meet for dinner, tomorrow night?" Dr. Morrow interjects.

Kristoff glares at him until he steps away.

"Is that it? Are you afraid of me?" He sounds torn up at the idea. I don't remember him caring much about my fear when he first met me.

"I'm not afraid. I've moved on from—" What? Our relationship? Stupid. "I'm moving forward, and I don't think we have anything to say to each other."

"You love me," he states like he's telling me I'm wearing shoes.

"What?" I can feel the heat in my cheeks and take a step back. "No. I cared for you because you showed me a very small amount of kindness in a really bad situation. After you made my life hell, I'll add. But no, I don't love you."

"You won't see the doctor I set up for you, or take the money that belongs to you, and you haven't moved into the apartment. How can I be sure your safe if you won't do what I tell you?" I see the little tick in his jaw and know he's getting upset, but he's holding himself steady.

"I don't need any of those things. I'm fine. I have a new job at a photography studio and I'm working on several projects on my own. I don't need your money or your help."

"You've been here every weekend for

two months, playing with someone," he says in the most jealous tone I've ever heard him use.

I smile. "Yes. An old friend."

"I don't like it," he admits, and I laugh.

"I'm not your prisoner anymore, Kristoff. You can't just pull up and demand I do everything you say. This is real life now. I have a life and I'm living it," I say, taking a long breath. Unless he wants to take me prisoner again. There isn't anyone on the street to stop him. It's late and the traffic is slow at this time of night.

The idea of being shuffled into his car shouldn't make me so damn tingly. But it does.

He takes a deep breath through his nose. "You're right. Let my driver take you home at least. I'll get another car."

"I just got here," I say.

"You're done for tonight." He shrugs. I suppose I should be happy he's not dragging me off to the car.

"And how do I know your driver won't just take me to some warehouse and lock me up?" I ask, half joking but mostly not.

His eyes darken. "You don't. But I give you my word, he'll drive you home." He's asking me to trust him. He abandoned me. If he'd wanted to keep me locked up in his basement, he wouldn't have gone through all the trouble of sending me back to the states in the first place.

Of all the things Kristoff has done to me, lying isn't one of them.

"You're not going to leave if I stay, are you?" I already know the answer.

"No, and if you go back inside to have some other man touch you while I'm standing here, I don't promise that I won't go in after you," Kristoff says with a grin. He knows he's winning.

"That's why Dr. Morrow went in?" I ask.

"He was afraid I'd lose my temper." Kristoff comes as close to rolling his eyes as I think he ever would. It's endearing.

I shake my head. I can't forget who and what he is.

"Is he your babysitter now?"

"He wanted to come with me to be sure you were healthy. He's here in an official capacity," Kristoff assures me, but after seeing Dr. Morrow's eyes roll, I know the truth. He's come to keep Kristoff under control. I don't think any man would have that power, but this doctor seems to have Kristoff's ear and heart.

I stare at him in silence. He's changed somehow, the anger I was so used to seeing simmering just below the surface isn't there anymore. He looks almost vulnerable while I'm deciding what to do.

Giving up, because I know he won't give in, I agree. "Fine, your driver can take me home. But I do have to go back in to tell Bobby I'm leaving and to grab my purse." I jerk a thumb at the door.

He raises an eyebrow. "Bobby?" he says the name with a forced American accent and I can't help but laugh. "This man who plays domination games with you is named Bobby?"

"Domination games?" I ask laughing again.

"Yes, it's a game here, yes? You play out fantasies and cuddle after?" His description isn't quite the full reality, but not too far off either.

"It's fun and safe," I say to him.

He shrugs. "Get your things and go home. Will you let me have dinner with you tomorrow?"

Will I let him?

I don't care for the term. He'd told me once I don't let anything happen where he and I are concerned. That felt more natural than this permissive conversation.

"Dinner? Sure. I can meet you—"

He shakes his head. "No. My driver will pick you up at seven o'clock. Don't be late, and don't wear that." He points to my dress. "Never wear that in public again. Burn the damn thing. I don't like it."

A black sedan pulls up behind the SUV and Kristoff waves to it. He really is taking a separate car.

"Men love this dress on me," I tease. I need to know where that line is, where is the Kristoff I met, and where is this man who stands in front of me.

"Exactly," he says with a raised brow and tense jaw. "They shouldn't need you to paint on your clothes to love you."

I want to question him about his statement. But he walks over to the second car and gets inside.

As it drives away, I simmer inside. He didn't even touch me, but my skin is hot.

"Well, that was odd," I say.

Dr. Morrow laughs. "Go get your things. I'll ride back with you since he's forgotten all about me."

I watch his car's taillights fade into the night. He's almost gentle now. Kind even.

I'm not sure I like it.

19

She's going to be a little pissed off when she gets here, but I can live with that.

It wasn't a lie about dinner, I just let her believe we'd be going out for the meal. Considering her first reaction to seeing me was to toss me to the side, I couldn't give her any reasons not to join me tonight.

I even cooked. Burnt everything, then ordered in, but I made the attempt. And I'm going to be damn sure she knows it. Because she deserves better than a monster, and I'm working to be that for her.

I tried to forget her over the past six months. When I found out, she rebuked every attempt at making sure she was okay, the only thing I could do was set her free. With men keeping tabs on her of course, but I didn't interfere.

KRISTOFF: BLAIRE'S WORLD

I know about her photography job, and I know she hates it. She's snapping family photos for shit's sake. And her little projects are puff pieces on the New York socialites. She's hiding from the world.

That stops now.

And if that means I have to go on dates with her to make it happen, I will. Because she deserves everything the world can give.

The front door of my condo overlooking Manhattan opens and I hear the click clop of heels on the tile. She's dressed up for me.

I step out of the kitchen to greet her. She's fucking gorgeous.

The dress she's wearing comes down to her knees, the neckline plunges enough for the swell of her breasts to show, and the dark green coloring is perfect for her skin.

"If I'd known we were staying in, I would have worn jeans," she says, wiping a loose hair from her eyes. She's left it down and curled it. It's longer than it was when we met, past her shoulders now.

"If you'd known we were staying in, you might not have come," I counter.

"True," she concedes. She looks around the condo. It's an open layout, the only two rooms that can't be seen are the bedroom and bathroom. "You live here now?"

"Only when I have to be in New York." Which gratefully isn't often. But if she lives here, I'll be spending more time.

"You cooked?" she asks leaning to see into the kitchen.

"In a way," I admit. "Burnt the spaghetti sauce, so I ordered food."

"You burnt spaghetti sauce?" she asks unbelieving. "I would think if you're going to cook, you'd cook something you're used to. Like something Russian?" She tosses her purse on the end-table and walks past the living area to the large windows showcasing the evening lights of the city.

"I thought you'd like spaghetti," I say. This feels wrong. Off somehow. Playful banter, casual talk. It's nauseating.

"Kristoff, why did you come here? I mean why now?" She turns to me, her hands fisted at her sides.

"I have a meeting—"

"No! I mean why did you find me? Why not just leave me alone?" she demands. Months ago, I wouldn't have allowed the tone, but this is different. I'm not on home ground here.

"You've never been alone," I admit. "I've known every move you've made since you were brought back home. I know where you work, what you eat for dinner most nights - which is spaghetti—" I point a finger at her. "I know you have one friend you see on Sundays for yoga, and I know you want to enjoy all this freedom, but you're not."

I'm taking a big chance here. If I'm wrong, she'll bolt, and I'll never get a second chance.

Her mouth opens then closes three times before she growls and turns back to the windows. "You are fucking impossible."

I smile. She didn't run.

"You are as stubborn as a fucking mule," I accuse.

"I want to forget you. I want to stop remembering all of it." Her voice softens, and her hand raises to her face.

She's crying.

"I'm sorry," I say, moving to stand just out of reach of her. If I get closer, I'll grab her and hold her and demand she never leave. This has to be her choice. She never had one with me before, but now she will. Even if she chooses to leave.

"I'm sorry for all of it - except for the part where you came into my life." I clear my throat. I'm not one for such talk, but it's the truth.

"My father's gone. His trafficking business dismantled along with him and most of his men." I want to assure her the men who hurt her died painfully, but I don't want her memory to trail down that lane.

"You're in charge now?"

"I am. You won't like what I do to earn my money. I'm not a good man. But there will be no more slaves bought or sold in my family name." The women my father kept in his clutches have all been given their freedom and have been set up with a life they will find some happiness in. "The estate in London has been sold. I won't be going back there again."

She tenses but doesn't speak.

I can't let her keep holding herself and thinking she's alone in this. I move forward, standing behind her and wrapping my arms around her body.

"You just left me. Sent me away like I was nothing," she whispers, twisting around in my arms and pressing her cheek to my chest. "You didn't want me, and I had made myself believe that in your own way - you did. I was wrong."

"No, you weren't wrong," I say, kissing the top of her head. "I was a fucking idiot. I needed to clean my house and I couldn't do that with you in it. I didn't want you to see me like that. I know I don't deserve you, I deserve nothing but the fiery flames of hell I'll surely meet when I die, but I can't help but want you."

"You kept tabs on me this whole time?" She pulls back to look up at me. Her eyes are red, the little mascara she wore has been smudged off. I run my thumb over her cheek to catch a tear.

"I wouldn't just let you go off into the world unprotected, and if you decide you don't want me, you'll always have my protection."

"And if I don't want that either?" She's pushing it, and I can see it in her eyes that she knows it.

"Well." I sigh. "You don't have a say in that."

"So, you'll always be hovering? And if I marry? Have kids?" She shoves away from me, but I catch her arm, holding her near me.

"It would kill me, but I would still make sure you were safe, all of them were safe," I vow.

"I don't know this Kristoff." She waves a hand at me. "This Kristoff is permissive, he's quiet. Undemanding."

"You'd rather have me force you?" I can't - won't do that again.

"No. Not that." She shakes her head. "You haven't even kissed me yet," she blurts out.

I was waiting for the right moment, for her to want it as much as me, but I see now what she needs. She needs my power, my strength. Not just armed guards, but me. She needs me.

KRISTOFF: BLAIRE'S WORLD

I yank her arm until back pressed against my chest again. Framing her face with both hands, I tilt her head back and crush her mouth with mine. My tongue doesn't beg entrance, but rather invades her and she tangles with me with as much force as always. She's not giving me an inch, she's making me take from her. And it's a sweet surrender when she finally places her hands on my chest and moans.

"This dress is better than that thing you wore last night, but I want it off," I say against her lips. My cock is bursting to get out of my pants, but I am determined to go slow with her. I won't hurt her a second time.

"What about dinner?" she asks, stepping out of my embrace.

"Fuck dinner," I say and step toward her, hunting my prey, and enjoying the chase she gives me when she moves away again. "The bedroom is that way." I point at the door she needs to go through to get to my bed. "But once you're in there, you lose your say. And you'll stay with me. No more department store photography, no more puff writing. You'll be mine."

She nods and keeps walking backward. I'm not running at her, but my heart is pounding like I've just sprinted up the stairs.

"Why is your dress still on?" I ask with a

determined step. "Are you back to being a naughty girl?"

KRISTOFF: BLAIRE'S WORLD

20

He's back. Kristoff is back, and the fire in his eyes and the deep tenor of his voice has sent shivers through my body. He stalks me to the bedroom, and I manage to get the dress off just as he pounces on me.

He lifts me into the air and tosses me on his bed. I bounce and laugh at the animalistic way he's acting, but I love it. I have craved it, and him for six long months.

"Panties?" he asks and grabs the elastic. "Never again," he announces and tears them off me. Good thing I left my bra at home, or he'd be ruining a very expensive panty set.

His shirt flies across the room, and he covers my body with his own. His hands are in my hair, tugging and holding me while his mouth claims mine again. I can barely breathe, but it doesn't stop me from matching him with my own aggression.

I reach down between us and pull at his belt.

He chuckles into my kiss. "Horny girl." He's called me a horny girl in Russian and I can't stop the smile from crossing my lips. I am that. Exactly that.

Getting to his knees on the bed, he pulls the belt open and works his zipper down before shoving his jeans off. I reach for him, wrapping my hand around the silky-smooth texture of his shaft.

"Oh, fuck." He groans and pulls my hand away. "You can't do that, love. I haven't had a woman since you left. If you do that, we won't get far."

His hands are everywhere, touching and pinching and rubbing me while his mouth moves from my lips to my cheek to my nipples. I arch my back when he licks my nipple into a beaded bud. Nothing has felt so good as his hands on me.

When his fingers find their way to my pussy, he pauses and looks up at me.

"Do you have any pain?" he asks with worry weighing down his words.

"No pain," I assure him. "I'm not breakable," I promise him and lift my hips to get his fingers to move.

He growls his intent before pushing two fingers inside of me. I hiss at the sudden full feeling and he tenses.

"Don't you fucking stop." I grab his shoulder and push him.

"Did you push me?" he asks with a devilish grin.

"No. I would never." I smile at him. I would if it meant he'd start moving his fingers, but I know what he's looking for. He's wanting my obedience, my submission. And I want to give it to him because it's his dominance that makes a safe place for me to hide. To be embraced and loved.

He spreads my legs and positions himself between them, stroking his cock over me and watching to be sure I'm seeing him. I can't tear my eyes away from his hand. I want him inside me. Not just my cunt, my entire soul.

"Please," I say and reach for him again, but he slaps my hand away.

"If you can't be good, you can't have any," he says and runs the head of his cock through my folds, gathering up all of my juices.

"Okay, okay," I say and put my hands at my sides.

He chuckles. "I may have found a new way to punish you." Before I can contest his comment, he thrusts into me in one quick push. I cry out, and he stills but I hug him.

"No. That's good. It's so fucking good." I

flatten my feet on the bed and arch my hips at him.

He holds nothing back now, he kisses me while he plows his thick length into me over and over again. I barely breathe or think. My heart hammers, but it's so loud in the room with his body slamming into mine, I can only feel it.

"Fuck. Oh fuck," he groans, his hands roaming over my breasts, then down between our bodies. "Come for me, Magdalena. Come hard, come for me," he chants and rubs my clit in a circle.

The pressure is too much, and I whine, but with one more thrust, one more flick of his finger it all explodes into a burst of white light and waves of pleasure that carry me away. I'm screaming out with each new thrust, driving my reward further and further until he plows forward once more and growls his own release into me.

My breath is shallow, my heart won't slow, and tears roll freely down my cheeks.

"Why?" he asks, out of breath himself, as he wipes the tears away.

"I thought you'd never come for me," I say and bury my head into his neck.

His cock slips out of me, making a mess across my thigh and his quilt, but he doesn't seem to care. He rolls to my side and pulls me to his chest.

"I'll always come for you." He hugs me tightly to him. "Always."

Silence stretches out between us, and I rest my chin on his chest. "You sure you can handle me like this? When I'm free to come and go as I please?"

"What makes you think you're free?" he asks and tweaks my nose.

"Because you aren't the monster you think you are."

"Oh, Magdalena, don't convince yourself otherwise. It would be dangerous to do so." I know he's telling the truth. The things he does for his business, for his money, they aren't good.

"No, you're not the monster with me. Me, you love." I press a kiss to his bare chest and rest my cheek against it, enjoying the steady rhythm of his heartbeat.

"You, I love," he agrees, and he tugs at my hair. "And you love me, too."

"Don't get a big head about it," I warn him, and he retaliates my snark with a quick smack to my ass.

"You still can be spanked and punished at my will. That doesn't change, Magdalena. You'll obey me, and you'll be a good girl, or you'll find I'm not as kind of a man you think me."

I move up to my elbows. "I would never insult you by thinking you're kind. But you won't hurt me, not really, not like before – like—" I take a deep breath. "You won't ever hurt me."

"No. I won't. And I will kill anyone who does."

I know he's not just saying these things. He doesn't threaten, he only warns before acting.

"Now is a good time for you to listen," he says, tightening his hold on me. "You will start to see the therapist Dr. Morrow went to the trouble to find for you, and you will claim the inheritance from your sister and trust next month when your birthday comes."

I want to argue, but his finger presses against my lips.

"If you don't want Danuta's money, donate it. Give it away, but don't let it just rot like she did."

He makes sense. I can put that money to good use, to help those that her actions may have hurt.

"Okay," I agree. "But I don't need the therapist," I press while he's being so giving.

"That's not open for discussion." He shakes his head and rolls me to my back. "I can always bind you to a chair and bring the doctor home for your appointments. But I think it would be a little counterproductive."

KRISTOFF: BLAIRE'S WORLD

He grins. He knows he's winning.
He always wins.
And now, with his arms wrapped around me, my life joining with his, I win, too.

THE END

Thanks for reading. I hope you've enjoyed **KRISTOFF**. If you could leave an honest review on Amazon and/or Goodreads, I'll be forever grateful.

I hope you will check out the rest of **BLAIRE'S WORLD:** 6 other Dark Romance Novels waiting just for you. They don't have to be read in any order, so you can dive right in wherever you'd like. All available on Amazon. Enrolled in Kindle Unlimited.

BLAIRE'S WORLD
BEAUTY
LUNA & ANDRES
DEMETRIUS
SERAFINA
EVELINA
OLIVER

I also encourage you to read **The Dark Romance Series** if you haven't already. With over 1000 5-star reviews, **BLAIRE**

and **BLAI2E** have become international Amazon sensations. Anna Zaires says BLAIRE, Part 1, is "Compelling Dark Romance."
Available on Amazon.
Enrolled in Kindle Unlimited.
Available on Audio.
Find them here: www.anitagrayauthor.com

OTHER BOOKS BY MEASHA STONE

Please visit meashastone.com

ABOUT **MEASHA STONE**

USA Today Bestselling Author Measha Stone is a lover of all things erotic and fun who writes kinky romantic suspense and dark romance novels. She won the 2018 Golden Flogger award in two categories, Best Advanced BDSM and Best Anthology. She's hit #1 on Amazon in multiple categories in the U.S. and the U.K. When she's not typing away on her computer, she can be found nestled up with a cup of tea and her kindle.

Printed in Great Britain
by Amazon